Praise for David H. Hendrickson

"A fantastic writer, one of our best working right now."

– Dean Wesley Smith,
USA Today bestselling writer

"David H. Hendrickson is one of my favorite writers."

– Kristine Kathryn Rusch,
USA Today bestselling writer

Praise for *Body Check*

Loved this. It's loaded with the authentic machismo of pro athletes and the honest struggles of a female sports journalist who's constantly negotiating all that testosterone. I got the feeling I was stepping behind the curtain of a sport (and a profession - sports journalism) I thought I knew and seeing what really goes on, and that was cool. And there was no doubt the two leads really cared for each other, which got you rooting for their happy ever after. Hendrickson's visceral writing style and sense of humor really sweep you along.

– Terry Hayman,
author of *Chasing the Minotaur*

Also by David H. Hendrickson

Novels: Romance

Body Check

No Defense

Novels: Young Adult-Sports-Historical

Cracking the Ice

Offside

Offensive Foul

Bottom of the Ninth

The Rabbit Labelle Trilogy (Omnibus)

Novels: Humor-Crime

Bubba Goes for Broke

Collections

Shimmers and Laughs: Eight Wildly Hilarious Tales

Death in the Serengeti and Other Stories: Ten Tales of Crime

The Boy in the Boxers and Other Stories of Sweet Romance

Hell of a Band: Twelve Fantasy Stories

Nonfiction

How to Get Your Book Into Schools and Double Your Income With Volume Sales

Travis Roy: Quadriplegia and a Life of Purpose

Romantic Concerto for Strings and Brass

DAVID H. HENDRICKSON

PENTUCKET PUBLISHING

Romantic Concerto for Strings and Brass

To Brenda,
the love of my life.
You're still the one!

Chapter One

Perfection. Anything less was unacceptable.

Standing in the sound room of her downtown Boston condominium, Julia Chu raised the priceless Stradivarius violin to her left shoulder, pinned it firmly in place with her delicate jaw, and after starting the recorded accompaniment, again began to play.

The Sibelius Violin Concerto. One of the most difficult pieces in the repertoire. A feature in this weekend's concerts and much of the upcoming tour.

Her fingertips flew across the fingerboard, modulating the pitch as she drew the bow across the strings in alternating short and long virtuosic strokes. The sweet, rich smell of the wood filled her nostrils, mingling with the sharper, pitch-like scent of the bowstring's rosin and the pungent odor of her own sweat. She had been practicing the Sibelius for more than four hours now, her long, straight, jet-black hair tied back in a ponytail and a gray sweatshirt, sweatpants, and running shoes substituting for her usual concert attire.

She planned to continue for at least another four hours. Or six or eight or ten.

Whatever it took.

Gray foam cushions covered the walls, soundproofing the twenty-

1

foot-by-twenty-foot sound room in her upscale Beacon Hill condo. The sound system, an audiophile's dream, played the orchestra's part in precisely the manner and details she expected the conductor, Maestro Joseph Rosenberg, would direct it to follow in the rehearsals prior to Friday night's performance. The acoustics would, of course, be different, as well as possible subtle interactions with the orchestra. That was what rehearsals were for.

But if you were one of the world's top three or four violin soloists with countless numbers of competitors snapping at your heels like ravenous, mad dogs—especially a few in Berlin and Vienna who were offended that yet another American had invaded their circles, stealing away a major recording contract and an upcoming world tour—you guaranteed perfection *before* the rehearsals.

Every day you guaranteed perfection. You practiced and practiced and practiced until the muscle memory was so fully ingrained in your body that if your heart stopped beating, the rest of your body would keep playing the Sibelius flawlessly.

That's what the rarified air of the concert violin soloist demanded.

Especially when you were a woman.

Ten years ago, when she was nineteen, the Parisian press had dubbed her *La Petite Fusée*, The Little Rocket, for the contrast between her tiny figure and her fiery style, and the name had stuck, though only after it had been hideously Americanized to *La Petite Rockette*, a name she abhorred because it conjured sex-drenched images of long-legged, short-skirted dancers tossing their stockinged bare legs high in the air as part of a Radio City Music Hall chorus line. But she had no power at the time to silence the name, and it suited the goals of her promoters, her eventual record label, and yes, even those who despised her and turned the term sneeringly into an affirmation of their claims of her unearned stardom.

At first, there had only been whispers. Eventually, though, those catty words to denigrate all she had accomplished became a harsh, braying chorus of hatred that Julia couldn't even pretend to ignore. Men and more than a few women, according to the haters, paid hundreds of dollars per ticket to attend her performances solely because of her physical attributes. Her pleasing, albeit petite, figure, her cover model's high cheekbones and flawless complexion, and her bright smile were what sold those tickets, not her matchless interpretation of the cannon of solo violin works.

"One need not be reminded that Chu rocketed up in the ranks of youth violinists while being judged by aging men found later to overtly favor pretty girls," one German magazine sniped. "Is she really superior to her European counterparts in anything other than America's most abundant export, superficial sex appeal?"

One scandal rag had even compared her full-length publicity photos and those shot by paparazzi over the years and claimed they proved Julia, not even five feet tall nor a hundred pounds, had undergone minor breast enhancement "to Americanize" her Chinese figure just prior to a record deal.

Which was absurd. She would no more change any part of her body close to where she tucked the violin beneath her chin and thereby risk even the slightest, most subtle impact on her playing than she would perform juggling stunts with the Stradivarius. Julia couldn't even imagine the diseased mind that would come up with such an allegation.

Social media was even more vicious. It had been blissfully nonexistent when her predecessors, Hilary Hahn and Sarah Chang, rose to stardom. They had been spared the venomous attacks from misogynists who could hide behind the veil of anonymous accounts. Predictably, the accounts spread rumors, depicted as verifiable facts, that she'd slept her way to the top. Slept with the youth judges and lecherous, influential conductors back when she was an under-eighteen talent. Slept with concert promoters all across the globe. Slept with the record company executives to get the deal.

She'd slept with none of them. Had, in fact, been forced to mandate a hands-off policy with those who became too handsy with her and had even lost out on opportunities to lesser talents because she had turned down carefully couched invitations to secure the position on her back.

She was far from a virgin. But she had always adhered to the maxim that you don't shit, pardon the language, where you eat. And you never, ever even consider desecrating the beauty of your art and cheapening the value of your accomplishments by gaining an edge in the bedroom. The vicious rumors were pure jealousy or the not-so-subtle sexism directed at women taking positions held in past generations by men. It couldn't be the abilities and insane drive for perfection that got a woman to the top. It had to be what was between her legs and how she exploited it.

Julia used the haters and gossipers to fuel her desire to become even better, if any further gasoline needed to be dumped on that inferno. She would be better today than yesterday. Better still tomorrow.

In every performance, she would show them all. She would prove her brilliance to the world. And to herself.

She would be perfect.

Friday night, three days later

Julia strode onto the Symphony Hall stage, the conductor in her wake and the ninety-five member orchestra seated off to her left. The men were dressed in traditional black tuxedoes with white ties and the women in equally conservative black dresses, unlike Julia, who wore an elegant lavender, silk, knee-length dress with rows of pleated ruffles to take away any hint of it fitting snugly to her skin. Her long hair was pulled back and held in place by an ornate, three-stone jade barrette that matched her half-finger-length, gold-and-jade earrings and necklace.

The applause was loud in expectation, though not thunderous. That would come at the end of the performance. If it didn't, then she had failed.

But Julia would not fail.

She would deliver perfection.

And she did. She blew the roof off the top of the venerable hall.

When the final note of the Sibelius sounded, the crowd stood and roared its adoration. Julia beamed her brightest smile and bowed. Pointed to the orchestra and Maestro Joseph Rosenberg and bowed again.

And yet still they roared.

Julia left the stage with Maestro Rosenberg only to be called back again. The audience required her appearance to shower her with even more praise.

The huzzahs went on and on. She was presented with a bouquet of flowers, bowed, left the stage, and was called back to take one more curtain call.

Nothing other than superficial sex appeal? Take that! Julia thought victoriously, even while noting deep in the back of her mind that taking a crowning moment like this and answering her critics instead of purely basking in the adoration tainted her achievement ever so slightly.

But she heard those critics in her mind, no matter how much she tried to silence them and enjoy this moment.

And she did enjoy the moment. How could anyone not delight in the roars of approval coming from the rafters on down to the orchestra, which was also applauding her feats.

Even more importantly, she heard her own silent standing ovation and huzzahs, for she knew she had nailed it. She had pleased her own harshest critic.

And to the rest of the critics, she had delivered an emphatic, though polite, fuck you.

Backstage in her dressing room, Julia wiped down the Stradivarius with one special smooth cloth for the wooden frame and then another to clean the rosin off the strings. Only after she had placed it under her own lock and key and in the Symphony Hall's safe did she wipe the beads of sweat off her own face with a plain white towel. Then, with a huge sigh, she took to reapplying her makeup for the tiresome meet-and-greet with the corporate sponsors of her upcoming tour that this performance was kicking off.

Twenty major American cities and then another twenty-five in Europe over almost a year. Even longer and with more performances than her past tours. It would be physically grueling and emotionally draining, moving from city to city, hotel to hotel, never having the ideal environment to maintain her sharpest edge in practice, yet demanding it nonetheless.

Even so, she couldn't wait for it all to unfold.

This was the pinnacle she had worked so hard to reach since beginning her lessons at the age of five and becoming a renown prodigy by the age of twelve, the only child of musical parents: her father, the former principal cellist for the Boston Symphony Orchestra, and her mother, the resident *prima donna* soprano for the Boston Opera Society.

Music was what she lived for.

For as long as she could remember, she'd held a violin and bow in her hands. Without her instrument, her hands felt empty.

Restless. Devoid of purpose.

And so she put up with the necessary evils, whether that be the critics or jealous rivals or events like this meet-and-greet with the sponsors. It was part of the life of a solo violinist, and she loved her life.

Julia peered into the mirror, finished prettying herself up—critics be damned, she needed to be pretty at times like this—then moved to the overly air conditioned open backstage area, perhaps forty feet by sixty, where the twenty-five or so corporate sponsors had gathered, waiting for her while contenting themselves with the maestro and lingering members of the orchestra.

All eyes turned to greet her when she entered the room, as was so typically the case, and then the sponsors, mostly older, balding men with large paunches and much younger, mostly blond, shapely wives broke into broad smiles and another road of enthusiastic applause. One ruffian, perhaps escaped from a rock or country music concert, sent a shrill whistle through the air.

Julia bowed and smiled, then pointed to them all as if they'd been performers, too, and watched them beam in approval.

This was ass-kissing, but all things considered, it wasn't bad at all.

Back at her condo, Julia slipped the Stradivarius softly into the safe next to her two lesser violins and four bows, showered, then went to the computer in her office. It sat in the middle of the large mahogany desk that dominated the room along with three-drawer gray filing cabinets in each of the far corners. A picture window looked out on a darkened Boston Common, now brightened only marginally by streetlights. Photographs of her posed with other famous musicians and directors, some now dead, filled almost every inch of the walls. Itzhak Perlman, Yo-Yo Ma, Claudio Abbado, Bernard Haitink, Pierre Boulez, Nikolaus Harnoncourt, and more.

Her father often joked that the collection would not be truly complete until it also included one of her with Paganini. For almost every audience, the joke didn't need the explanation that Paganini had died in 1840.

But Paganini, Perlman, Ma, and the others were of no concern to her right now. Though it was after midnight, she was still wired to the gills. Adrenaline still rushed through her veins.

As it always did after big performances like tonight.

It necessitated the means she used, on occasions such as tonight, to release the pressure cooker of steam that had been building and building and building for the many days and weeks leading up to this night.

She went online, double-checked her selection, then verified the reservation made weeks earlier at the luxurious Top of the Charles hotel next door.

Julia wasn't just ready to blow off steam.

She was *ready*.

Chapter Two

The smells of Italian sausage with peppers and onions, knockwurst, pizza, and cheeseburgers floated through the chilly October air. Midway barkers called to passersby, offering them chances to win ever increasingly large stuffed animals, all the way up to the ten-foot-tall white polar bear, its arms stretched out wide.

"Step right up. Two shots for a dollar! Five for two!" they called. "Get the ball in the center and win a prize! Step right up!"

Nearby, bells clanged as other contestants squirted water from a water gun into a plastic clown's mouth which, when hit squarely in the middle, propelled six-inch Indy-style racing cars to the top for a prize.

Tilt-A-Whirl rides spun, Ferris Wheels rotated, and the Flying Bobs dipped and swerved around and around, the ride conductor occasionally interjecting instructions in the middle of music that blared "Shook Me All Long," "Welcome to the Jungle," and "Bad to the Bone."

The Topsfield Fair was the longest running fair in America, held in the partly rural, partly suburban bedroom town of Topsfield, forty minutes north of Boston. It also featured 4-H club exhibits, greased pole competitions, the freakishly sized world's largest pig, so rotund it appeared to only be able to lie on its side, and outrageously sized vegetables: award-winning pumpkins the size of dining room tables and watermelons weighing more than a hundred pounds.

Slavko Novak and his band had played at similar state fairs across the country, especially in their home state of Wisconsin and throughout Pennsylvania, upstate New York, and Ohio, totaling more than two hundred performances a year. Been there, done that, as the saying went. Even so, Slavko still felt a pang of unease as they stepped onto the elevated stage off the midway, wearing their trademark plaid red-and-white flannel shirts in front of a matching backdrop bearing the band's name. He looked out onto the forty-foot-wide by eighty-foot-deep tented, grassy area lined with twenty rows of metal folding chairs behind a spacious area up front set aside for couples to dance.

A perfect venue, missing only one thing.

An audience.

Again.

All those perfectly aligned rows of folding chairs were empty, save for a single elderly, white-haired couple in the very last row on two end seats, a position seemingly chosen to allow for a quick exit.

An audience of two.

Slavko, a broad-shouldered, barrel-chested man of thirty-one just under six feet tall and with thick, dark, wavy hair parted on the side, maintained a frozen smile on his face. But it was a struggle. In theory, he and the boys would begin to play and fans old and new would arrive to take their seats and in no time the dancing and merriment would be in full swing.

That was the theory. The reality had been quite different far too often.

The Pied Piper Polish Polka Dots had earned worldwide fame amongst polka aficionados, totaling nine nominations for International Polka Association awards and five wins, all for Slavko individually. There was no one better on the tuba and in his own humble way, he was intensely proud of that. Tuba playing involved a lot more than *oompah, oompah* all throughout the song. He attempted to provide a more melodic approach than was typical with the bass notes he laid down, much like Paul McCartney had decades ago on the bass guitar with the Beatles and then solo. Slavko would never speak such prideful words aloud, of course, but clearly his peers agreed. He felt honored every time they recognized his finely crafted skills. And he never felt more alive than when he hoisted that twenty-eight-pound piece of gold-colored brass magic, clipped in his shoulder strap, and made listeners happy.

Sadly, though, that joy of performing and the acclaim of his awards along with two bucks would buy him a cup of coffee. The band was a big fish in the tiny pond of polka, but if Slavko was being honest with himself, that tiny pond had become in recent years little more than a shallow puddle. And the shallow puddle was drying up fast, leaving the big fish that they were flopping around without air.

The Polka Dots weren't just teetering on the brink of insolvency. They were one blown engine or transmission from going over the edge. A year ago, two of the other three original members had left the band for what they called *real jobs*. "You know, the kind that pay enough to live on," had been their parting comment. Not meant maliciously; just stating an undeniable fact. It had left only Slavko on tuba and his boyhood friend, Happy Eddie, a dead ringer for a rotund Santa Claus, playing the accordion and adding in vocals when needed. They added two replacements—the skin-and-bones duo of Junior Kowalski on trumpet and Silent Wally Yablonski on clarinet—and set off on what Slavko privately called the "Make It or Break It Tour."

They were breaking it.

They were shattering into so many pieces, Slavko feared the band would, like Humpty Dumpty, never get back together again. Just two weeks earlier, a string of cancellations and broken promises on the part of bar owners had forced Slavko to cut everyone's pay temporarily, himself included. In fact, he'd taken a deeper cut than anyone else despite being the band's leader, manager, and inarguably its star. He was as dead broke as the rest of them.

What was he supposed to do? Put the bills on the corporate American Express? There was no corporate American Express. There was no cash. There was, quite possibly, no hope. Nonetheless, he'd faced a near mutiny when he announced the pay cuts, temporary until they could get back on their feet. Even Happy Eddie had appeared on the verge of deserting Slavko.

They desperately needed full crowds this weekend. The fair's management, faced with a last-minute cancellation of a popular local band, had been dubious about giving the three prime weekend dates to a *polka band*. The words had been spoken with an audible sneer to go with the Bostonian accent. *Polka? You've got to be joking.* Slavko had gotten the gig for the band only by agreeing to a low base pay with bonuses based on crowd size. A gamble, but the best he could do.

They had an audience of two.

Two, hanging on the periphery ready to bolt.

Slavko maintained his frozen smile, gave an earnest, enthusiastic welcome to their crowd of two, and silently begged the gods of music for a break.

Please. Just a few fans. Or people who've never heard of us or given polka a second's thought. Just give us a chance.

The Pied Piper Polish Polka Dots launched into its playlist of almost twenty songs, featuring their hits "Rock and Rye Polka," "Out of My Mind Polka," "Wedding Wreath Waltz," "Cuckoo in the Clock Polka," and of course their trademark song, "Pied Piper Polka." But even as the chilly October evening air gusted, bringing with it the familiar smells of sausage and bratwurst from nearby cooking stands, the hoped-for flock of listeners did not come.

The elderly, white-haired couple remained throughout, bless their hearts. They even moved up front to dance the polka and clap their hands with glee. Thank God for them, Slavko thought, and a few others from the over-fifty crowd that arrived and stayed for a song or two. Almost everyone else, however, who poked their heads inside the tented area rolled their eyes and shook their heads before moving on. Or even worse, lingered only to ridicule.

The worst moment of all came, ironically, when the band played "Beer Barrel Polka," the most popular polka of all. A half dozen teenagers appeared, four boys and two girls, prompting Slavko to give a jubilant eye to the other band members. *About time! Here we go!*

The teenagers, however, broke into song, drowning out Happy Eddie's vocals.

> *Roll on you Bulldogs.*
> *Show them how you got your name.*
> *Roll on you Bulldogs.*
> *Each game enhances your fame.*
> *Fight on to victory.*
> *You're not afraid of your foe.*
> *The courage of the English Bulldogs,*
> *Everybody knows!*

And then they all left, laughing and slapping each other on the back, yelling out snide remarks. They'd hijacked the performance to sing their school's fight song, then left. Where Slavko had foolishly thought the band had engaged some enthusiastic fans—finally!—and younger ones to boot, it had instead attracted only more ridicule.

As they left the stage, the degrading night mercifully over, Slavko could see the humiliation on the faces of the boys. They ducked behind the red-and-white plaid backdrop and took a set of steps down to the grassy ground, crestfallen, their shoulders slumped. Though they always tried to hide their emotions and present a cheery front to the audience, those masks had fallen now. Junior, rail-thin and just turned twenty-one while the rest of them were in their early thirties, looked like he'd just learned of a death in the family. A haunted look covered his otherwise boyish, fuzzy-cheeked, scrawny face.

Which was exactly how Slavko felt inside.

To be a musician was to invite low moments. A million songs had been written about that reality. You had to swing with the punches and when you got knocked down, get right back up. No one was going to feel sorry for you.

But it still stung, and Slavko could see it on the other members' faces every bit as much as he felt it in his own wounded heart. Even the almost-always-jovial Happy Eddie couldn't hide his feelings. He looked like the world's most miserable Santa Claus.

"Hey, we'll turn things around tomorrow night," Slavko said, but immediately realized he'd have been better off saying nothing. It had been the world's worst pep talk, the words hollow, bordering on ludicrous.

The looks he got back told him the boys didn't believe his groundless, cheery optimism for a second.

And truth be told, neither did he.

Slavko pulled the Ford Explorer SUV into the parking lot of the Motel 6, the band's plaid red-and-white trailer holding the band's equipment in tow. Less than five miles from the fairgrounds, they checked into a single room with two double beds. They flipped for it, and Slavko and Happy Eddie each got a queen-size bed. Silent Wally and Junior would take the floor tonight. Tomorrow, the roles would be reversed.

After a shower and a quick check on his phone to confirm the details of the evening's plans, Slavko headed into Boston alone. His expectations were lower than low. He'd set up a DiscreetPartnerForYou account in a fit of dark loneliness but was regretting it already. This wasn't his kind of thing at all.

$$Chapter\ Three$$

When the knock came on the door to her hotel suite, Julia was ready. Hell, she'd been ready since the cheers cascaded down on her from the cheap seats at Symphony Hall and radiated upwards from the expensive orchestra section.

Ready.

The pressure had built and built and the need for release grown and grown, and now she was...

More than ready.

The knock came on time, but the heat had been building and building until she could barely stand it. Her heart pounded, though she was not nervous, but her hands quivered ever so slightly as she looked at herself in the mirror.

She hardly recognized herself. Gone was the subtle, almost skin-colored makeup, the elegant jewelry, stage clothing, and jet-black hair tied back.

In its place was makeup for her high cheekbones of a darker hue. Heavy application of eye shadow. Bright red lipstick. A flowing, rust-colored wig. Bookish-looking fake glasses and contact lenses that turned her normally soft brown eyes the brightest blue.

And that was just the start.

A short black fuck-me skirt and high spiked heels. A white blouse sheer enough to show the outline of her hard nipples.

So unlike the beautiful but ever-so-proper image she exuded to the public.

She felt a brief pang of sadness that her love life was reduced to this, that her relentless pursuit of artistic perfection—the only way to get to the very top in the cutthroat world she lived in—excluded a real relationship. Real relationships took time and effort, inevitably subtracting from the tunnel-minded obsession it took to become world class and then stay there. She'd found that out the hard way years ago.

For her, a conventional love life was impossible. You had to make your choices and live with them. Yet even the most isolated, dedicated artist required a salve for her loneliness. Denied a real relationship or even the ease of a casual fling achieved in a public hookup at anything from a cheap bar to a high society fundraiser—just begging to be exposed as a scandalous tart—Julia's options came down to lonely celibacy or an occasional discreet, anonymous liaison like this.

And so it was. This was the life she'd chosen and she regretted it not one bit. She'd climbed to the top of her artistic mountain and was proud of it. If others thought they could look down on her and even be aghast at this tawdry activity, Julia didn't care. To hell with them.

As long as they never found out.

What the public didn't know wouldn't hurt them. And Julia was intent on them never knowing. She would maintain her squeaky clean image. But she was equally intent on filling the loneliness in her heart and satisfying her most intimate longing for a man.

She was going to make the most of this night. She felt like a lioness hungry to devour her next meal. *Grrrr.*

She was *ready.*

Julia dimmed the lights. She'd disguised herself as much as she could, but perhaps no makeover could conceal her identity. With heart pounding, she stepped to the door and peeked in the peephole.

"Please identify yourself," she said. Peepholes being what they were, she really couldn't see much of the man, but he gave the proper code word specified by DiscreetPartnerForYou, indicating that he'd been vetted. No names or any other identifying information would be exchanged, maximizing confidentiality.

Julia opened the door with the safety chain still attached, poked her head around, and verified that the man was alone.

Alone and drop-dead gorgeous.

Not quite six feet tall, but that was okay since she was barely five even. Broad athletic shoulders. Barrel-chested. Wavy dark hair and a nice smile. A blue dress shirt and tight jeans. A leather jacket slung over his arm.

The perfect boy toy. A mouthwatering piece of eye candy, and one who wanted to play the innocent shy virgin, manipulated by his seducer, told what to do and how to do it. As many times as she wanted. Over and over, as long as he could still perform, she could use him wantonly for her pleasure. That, according to the website, would be his own pleasure.

There would be no emotion. Absolutely no emotion. Purely physical. If they kissed, it would only be for the sensual delight of lips touching lips. Nothing more than raw sexual pleasure.

Julia couldn't wait to devour him.

She unlatched the door and, heart thumping, let him inside.

"Can I get you a drink?" she asked.

He smiled, showing a dimple in his chin. Julia liked dimples.

"I'll have one if you're having one," he said. "But I don't need anything. It's up to you."

That was the right answer.

***

She led him to the dimly lit bedroom and all but threw him on the king-size bed and tore off all his clothes. She didn't actually pop any buttons on his shirt as he lay there flat on his back, but she came close. She also didn't break his belt buckle or the zipper before yanking his tight jeans off of him and casting them roughly aside. But she sure came close.

She ran her fingertips along his bare skin. Across his face, his almost totally hairless, broad chest, along the flatness of his abs, and down his legs. Julia bent over and licked his left nipple and then the right, caressing his side, then playing with the nipples.

Her sleek boy toy. Hers to command.

Nice.

She kicked off her spiked high heels. They fell with a dull clunk upon the thickly carpeted floor. She took one hand of his and slid it inside her sheer white blouse, then felt warmth course through her as he smiled and caressed her small breasts, playing with the already-hard nipples.

She took his other hand and slid it up her skirt.

"Feel me up," she said huskily, then guided his hand inside her black lace panties to her wetness.

Yes. Yes.

He explored for a time with boyish enthusiasm, and after she moved his hand to the right position, he fingered her clitoris. Side to side. Up and down. All around.

Yes. Yes.

There would be no making love tonight. This would be raw, pounding animal sex. Just the way she liked it.

Just the way he liked it, too, if DiscreetPartnerForYou could be believed, and it had been dead-on right so far. Not that she really cared. This man would get the time of his life as a byproduct of her own insatiable lust, getting his pleasure from servicing her.

And he *would* service her.

She intended to be the most selfish of lovers, letting her passion explode from her like a steaming fiery-hot volcano and in the process envelop him with the passion he enjoyed most.

Raw animal sex. And she was the fucking alpha.

"Take my clothes off," she commanded.

He unbuttoned her blouse and slid it off her shoulders, his fingertips sliding across her skin. Then, with her moving so he could pull them off, her skirt and panties. Last of all, because she had forgotten them, the fake glasses.

They faced each other on the bed, naked, Julia on her knees near his hips and him lying there with that soft, innocent smile.

An innocent smile she could get used to.

Julia quickly banished that thought from her mind and brushed her lips against his. Kissing them. Sweet and soft. Tasting of spearmint.

Nice.

So she kissed them again. Nicer still.

And still that innocent, virgin smile, as if this were his first time, though it most certainly was not. That innocent smile and his dark green eyes. So one more time she kissed him.

Not exactly raw animal sex. But she liked a kiss or two or three. Just not too many. Too many and there was just the slightest chance of making more of this than what it was.

Two animals rutting. Sating their lusts.

Thrusting and heaving and sucking and grabbing. The seductress and her innocent.

And so she kissed him one last time, lingering as he slipped on a condom as she ordered. She enjoyed the lingering because he really did have the softest virgin lips, so sweet and soft and minty. And what was surely his cologne smelled pleasingly of cedarwood with the slightest hint of nutmeg and citrus.

She swung one leg across to the other side of his hip, mounting him, and then slid his hardness inside her. She sank down on him all the way, ground her hips, then lifted them slowly.

Up and then all the way down his hardness. Up and down. Up and down.

Grinding herself against him, the pressure on her clitoris sending shivers up her spine. Grinding and grinding. Then up and slamming down on his hardness.

She'd thought she'd go slowly for a time, not rushing it, but soon her passion and all the steam built up inside her overrode that plan.

She rode him like a wild-ass bronco until her pleasure built and built and then built some more. Finally, it erupted in an orgasm that all but shot off fireworks inside her head as it washed over her in huge crashing waves, forcing her to scream out in delight so loudly it surely could be heard as far away as Symphony Hall.

When he appeared spent and Julia was all but sated, she decided that her sweet little virgin boy toy wasn't as spent as he might think. She lifted herself off him, saw his hardness failing fast beneath the condom, then took the warm wet facecloth she'd left on the nightstand atop a towel and dabbed between her legs.

"Not done yet, my darling," she said.

She kissed him, stroked his cheek, and smiled back at his wide, innocent boyish grin, a grin for which she felt an almost magnetic attraction. A grin she could get very used to. *Used to.* The temptation flashed though her mind and pierced her heart for the briefest instant before, alarmed, she banished it from all consciousness. What had she been thinking? She knew better than to view this boy toy as anything more than just that.

A boy toy, nothing more. Boy toy. Boy toy. Boy toy.

Julia blinked every other thought away. *Boy toy.* She moved until she was kneeling almost beside his head that lay flat against the covers. She lifted a leg over to the other side of his head, and facing the wall, away from his body, lowered herself down upon his face.

"Eat me!" Julia commanded.

The boy toy complied. Wonderfully complied. Her sweet boy toy did stunning things with his tongue, mouth, and lips. Licking, sucking, and kissing.

Stunning!

She lowered herself down on him more forcefully, and with an expertise with which she'd never been orally serviced before—*never!*—he pleasured her even as she ground herself into his face, his tongue, mouth, and lips, barely letting his mouth escape for an occasional breath.

Her body shook with pleasure.

And for the second time, though with a different part of his body to delight her, she once again rode her boy toy like a wild-ass bronco.

Chapter Four

Slavko had heard of men being thunderstruck by a woman. Seen it in the movies. The Michael Corleone character from *The Godfather* when he was exiled to Sicily. One look was all it took. But Slavko had dismissed it as romantic nonsense. Silly. Absurd. Fanciful foolishness. He had certainly never felt anything like it. Never even considered it possible.

Until now.

Thunderstruck. It was the only way to describe the instant bolt that shot through him when the Chinese goddess opened her hotel room door. Even with what were obvious attempts to disguise her identity—a rust-colored wig, bookish glasses, and garish red lipstick—she was the most beautiful woman he'd ever seen. And that was before the raw sexuality of the sheer white blouse, the black miniskirt, and high spiked heels.

But somehow it was even more than that. She radiated something special, a magical aura of some kind, something indefinable.

She was a goddess.

Not surprisingly, he hadn't lasted all that long the first time, which was hardly a shock since this was easily the most mind-blowing sex of his life. Not that there'd been much in the way of competition. Despite being an accomplished musician and exceptionally popular in the small world of polka music, he'd always been naturally shy and reserved with women. He felt painfully awkward walking up to a stranger in a bar and trying to make conversation. It just seemed so...forward and aggressive.

Hey, baby, what's your name?

Slavko could no more do that than he could play tuba and sing at the same time. It just wasn't him. And the polka world was far at the other end of the spectrum from rock and roll with its seemingly limitless supply of willing young flesh throwing themselves at its stars.

So on a lark, he'd signed up for the online service and hit a grand slam home run all the way to the moon and beyond in this his first try. His lack of experience and innate shyness had made his innocent virgin role playing as easy to follow as seemingly Jack Nicholson's was of a maniacal wild man in *The Shining*. After the first minute or two, Slavko had just been himself, lying on the huge, king-size bed in the beautiful woman's hotel suite, letting her guide his hand first inside her blouse to play with her hard nipples and then into her black lace panties.

"Feel me up!" she'd said in a husky, mind-blowing whisper.

Slavko hadn't needed to be told twice. He responded with enthusiasm, especially after she guided his hand to her wetness and then her clitoris and responded to his touch, moving her hips in an almost hypnotic rotation.

When she mounted him and slid her slick, tight sex up and down his shaft, he gasped with pleasure, gazing in wonder at her petite beauty, caressing her hips as they ground against him, and trying desperately to make it last.

She exploded in exuberant pleasure just before he did, but that didn't stop her from quickly cleaning him off, applying a new condom, and picking up exactly where she'd left off.

She rode him hard, lifting herself up almost to the tip of his cock before slamming herself back down on him.

Up and down. Up and down.

Then grinding herself upon his pelvis, rocking back and forth so her clit could rub against him.

And then she lifted herself up off him almost to the point where he cried out because he feared she would separate herself from him, and then at the very peak of his cock, she slammed herself fiercely down.

Gorgeous and athletic in her sexuality. Moaning and gasping. Guiding his hands to her breasts, then his thumb to her clit.

Crying out with her pleasure. Loud and intense. Over and over.

Slavko began to think it was all a dream. This couldn't be happening to him. He couldn't possibly be giving this creature sent down from the Greek god Eros this much pleasure.

And then, he couldn't hold back any longer. His eyes involuntarily shut and he thrust his hips upward to meet hers. He gripped her hips tightly, thrusting and thrusting. He willed his eyes back open so he could look at her, needing to see her to be sure this dream was reality.

They cried out together and the explosion seemed to last forever and ever.

She collapsed on him, her head resting on his neck. Slavko smelled the strawberry scent of her hair mixed with the scents of their lovemaking. He felt the sweat upon her skin mingling with the sweat on his own heaving chest. Their bodies trembled in unison, singing the song of exhausted delight.

After a time, she lifted herself off him and applied one towel to her own sex and cleaned him off for a second time with another, tossing the used condom aside.

He was done. Used up. Consumed totally.

And how wonderful it had been. Slavko's head spun with satisfaction and lingering disbelief. *He* had made this astonishing creature moan and shriek and gasp with delight.

Him!

Her!

It boggled his mind. Filled him with wonder and amazement.

But there would be no more pleasure tonight. He would have to ask her about another rendezvous tomorrow or the night after, his last nights in Boston. And perhaps somehow, though it was surely impossible based on pure geography, after that in the weeks and months to come. Not just more coupling, even though that had been beyond his wildest imagination. Perhaps a romantic dinner in which they discussed their likes and dislikes, their hopes and dreams. Or maybe just a movie, holding hands and eating buttered popcorn. Whatever she wanted.

He wasn't just thunderstruck by her beauty. He wasn't just thunderstruck by her sexual prowess. He was thunderstruck by that indefinable magical aura of hers.

Of course, he would love to please her more tonight if his body allowed. But there was no life left in his penis. This time, his penis had quickly shrunk. He had been drained dry. There would be no more servicing of this supremely erotic, amazing creature. Except...

"Not done yet, my darling," she said.

She kissed him and stroked his cheek with her fingertips. Slavko grinned sheepishly, afraid to tell her that he was indeed done. There was nothing left in him.

Except...

She moved up to crouch beside his head. Then she lifted a leg over to the other side of his head, straddling it, facing away from his body, and lowered herself upon his face.

"Eat me!" she commanded.

For only the briefest instant, he sensed just a trace scent of the rubber condoms, but then the musky aroma of her sex overwhelmed him. He delighted in its wetness even before he put his mouth and lips on her, kissing her most intimate area, licking it, sucking on it.

Then kissing it even more feverishly. Licking more feverishly. Sucking more feverishly.

Loving it more feverishly.

"*Oh, yes!*" she screamed. "*Yes!*"

Slavko had spent a lifetime developing and perfecting his tuba-playing embouchure, making the use of his lips and surrounding muscles world-class. Based on the woman's screams of delight, Slavko thought that, inexperienced or not, his ability to give oral pleasure just might, to his amazement, be world-class as well.

"*Yes! Right there! Yes!*" she screamed.

Slavko used those world-class muscles with even more enthusiasm and she responded in kind.

"*Oh my God! Yes!*"

She ground her hips down on his mouth and lips, crying out in pleasure, urging him on.

"*Yes! Yes!*"

Out of control, she pressed herself so fiercely on his face that she cut off his air supply at times, but Slavko didn't let that interrupt her pleasure. He let her scream out her delight and encouragements. There was nothing more exciting, he was finding, than a woman totally out of control with sexual bliss, the orgasms rolling over her time after time.

So he drew on the exceptional lung capacity he'd developed over the years of tuba playing. Where a lesser man might panic, thinking he was about to pass out or get asphyxiated as she squeezed herself hard against his face, grinding her hips in delight, cutting off air to both mouth and nose for long stretches, Slavko serviced her joyfully.

He looked up from below her, his hands resting atop the soft skin of her upper thighs, and watched in amazement and astonished delight as she arched her back, exposing those wonderfully petite breasts and so very hard nipples, throwing back her head in ecstasy and crying out with the pleasure that *he* was giving her.

Over and over.

He was doing this for *her*!

It defied imagination.

The views of the Grand Canyon, Mount Everest, and every scenic sight in between had nothing on the sight of her pleasure. Nothing could match the delight he felt as her body shook with the purest sexual bliss.

And when she finally lifted herself off his face for good, he saw that his penis had, of course, sprung back to life, standing at full attention in salute to her. And one final time, with a fresh condom applied, she moved her magnificent body down on top of that rock-hard erection instead of his face, and once again drained him dry.

Slavko held her still-trembling body in his arms, smelling the strawberry scent of the hair beneath her obvious wig. She had slid the lower half of her body off him and onto the bed but her head was nestled pleasantly against his neck and her arms were draped across his shoulders, their moist chests still skin to skin. Slavko caressed her hip and side. He kissed the top of her head, then the side of her neck and her bare shoulder.

"Holy shit!" she gasped, propping herself up to look at him. "How did you do that? With your mouth, I mean. That was amazing."

Slavko smiled. Were there any better words in the English language? In any language?

But since secrecy was the code word of the website through which they met, he decided to answer the astonishing creature's questions with one of his own.

Heart pounding, he looked into her bright blue eyes. "Can I see you again?"

"Tomorrow night," she said instantly.

Her eyes widened, almost comically, as if surprised at her own words.

"I mean..." she said, then blinked and shook her head as if trying to clear her mind. She took a deep breath. "I guess that would be okay."

Okay? Just...okay?

Slavko's shoulders slumped. The air rushed out of his lungs and he could barely breathe, decades of tuba playing behind him or not. He felt crushed, and wanted to ask, "Just okay?" but his lips wouldn't form the words.

Apparently, he was the only one who was thunderstruck.

She laughed gently. "I didn't mean it that way." She stroked his cheek with the tips of her fingers. "I'm just...I'm just a very private person and don't usually..." She shook her head. "In fact, I can't believe I even said yes. Even though you were amazing. What you did orally...I've never..." A groan escaped from her lips in obvious amazement.

Slavko beamed.

"Same time tomorrow," she said. "Right here."

Slavko smiled with satisfaction and kissed her soft lips. She hesitated for a moment, but then responded hungrily. Greedily. She ran her fingers through his hair, devouring his lips with ever more feverish kisses.

He hoped this would never stop. Wanted it to last forever.

Suddenly she pulled away and rolled off him. A split second later, she stood beside him.

"Don't be late," she said in what he knew were words of dismissal.

Slavko smiled, though he wished he could stay.

He was no fool. He wouldn't be late. There was no chance of *that* happening.

Chapter Five

Julia slipped back inside her condo, wearing the same plain gray, baggy jogging suit, old sneakers, baseball cap, and oversized sunglasses she'd worn hours ago when she left. She stepped inside her bedroom closet and dropped the nondescript gray duffle that held her makeup kit and other clothes—the sheer silk blouse, the short black skirt, and the spiked high heels—then quickly brushed her teeth and slipped into bed.

She stared at the ceiling, still feeling the tingle of pleasure between her legs, still seeing her boy toy's captivating smile.

What the hell had she done? Her rule had always been one night and one night only. No exceptions. To spend a second night with a man was just asking for trouble. It didn't just double the chances of being identified; it multiplied them a hundredfold or more. Not to mention the possibility of a messy emotional entanglement.

Not from her end, of course. She felt a tug in her heart for her innocent boy toy with the astounding oral skills and had even been foolishly responding to his loving kisses after they both were sexually spent. It had taken her far too long to stop that dangerous act, belatedly pulling away and jumping to her feet as if stung by a bee. She'd be sure not to make that mistake in their return rendezvous and of course, would excise that nugget of aching in her heart right this instant as if it were a cancerous growth.

She'd never allow her heart to destroy her again.

Never.

She'd learned that lesson the hard way back when she was seventeen and foolish. She'd fallen hard for a boy, a Chinese boy that her parents approved of and a prodigy cellist, no less. His name had been Xiangyu Lee, slender with short black hair and the brightest smile she had ever seen.

A smile he shone on her. Beaming.

She loved him with a passionate fury and within a few months they took each other's virginity with sweaty, fumbling enthusiasm in the back seat of his parents' SUV. As Xiangyu entered her, Julia knew they would spend the rest of eternity knowing only each other. There would be no other lovers for either of them. Only each other from the beginning to the end. The sweetest of fairy tales. The most romantic of all romances.

The two innocents intertwined forever as one.

Eventually to become husband and wife.

Wedded bliss.

The next day, however, Xiangyu wouldn't even look at her. And when Julia asked him what was wrong, he told her coldly that he could never marry a woman who wasn't a virgin on their wedding night. She was ruined now in his eyes. They would share no future together.

In their months together, Julia had allowed her violin practice to slip ever so slightly as her thoughts and attentions had become more wrapped around Xiangyu. She had still practiced every day, of course, but fifteen minutes or even a half hour that could have been spent on her craft had gone to calling him on the phone or even just thinking about him and dreaming about their eventual life together.

When he crushed her with his icy rejection, Julia fell apart. Huge wracking sobs of grief consumed her for days, eventually giving way to sniffling tears. For weeks, she wanted nothing to do with music.

To hell with the violin. To hell with it all.

She was a ruined woman. Xiangyu had been right about that. Her life was over.

But then, two months to the day that he had ruined her, the cruel bastard won a national cello competition. Two weeks later, his gorgeous, smiling, heartless face filled *The Boston Globe* Living/Arts feature section.

The headline read: *The Next Great One*

Not a question. A statement of fact.

Inside the story, sparing no false humility, Xiangyu spoke of his dreams of greatness and of world tours where he could play in the same cities where Bach and Beethoven created the works he was playing.

The very same dreams Julia had held. The same desires that had burned like a fiery furnace inside her heart.

Until he'd hijacked them.

He hadn't stolen her dreams and taken them as his own, of course. They were the dreams of most classical musicians her age. Xiangyu had held them, too, before he stole her heart. They had shared those same musical desires before they also shared each other's carnal desires.

But only he had emerged from the wreckage of their relationship with those dreams still intact. His casual destruction of her—"I could never marry a woman like you"—had applied a wrecking ball not only to how she looked at herself but also to her own dreams of greatness.

Because she had let him.

He hadn't hijacked her dreams along with her self-worth. *She* had allowed him to do so. And she could deliver the only "fuck you" possible to that heartless bastard by taking them back.

The Next Great One? It wouldn't be Xiangyu on his goddamned cello. It would be her, Julia Chu, the next great solo violinist. The greatest of her era, maybe even the greatest of all time.

And so Julia picked the violin back up again. At first, it felt like a stranger in her hands. For a time, she could not control the rage with which she played it. Her passion flared even during soft passages that spoke of peace and tranquility, a tranquility she could not recognize.

But eventually the violin once again became her most intimate, trusted lover. She held it in her hands as if it were an extension of herself, which, in fact, it was. Hours upon hours of practice passed, days upon days, weeks upon weeks. The beauty of Mozart, Beethoven, and Bach flowed through her fingers. The Tchaikovsky Concerto. The Sibelius. And the aching beauty of the second movement of the Brahms.

The violin was once again her first love. Not Xiangyu, that foolish little boy. To hell with him.

Julia had fallen back madly in love, head over heels, ass over teakettle, with her violin. Hardly a day went by without at least four hours of practice. Most days, much more. The fingers on her left hand yearned for the touch beneath their tips of the thin fretless string; the fingers on her right hand longed for the firmness of the bow. The thirst for more time to play, for more time with this instrument of her greatest pleasure, became insatiable.

That desire underlined just how foolish she had been to let Xiangyu derail her from her true destiny. To distract her from her first love.

She had been an unfaithful lover, she knew now, when she had allowed herself to be seduced by the emotional entanglements of a mere foolish boy. It had almost cost her everything. In a sense, Xiangyu had done her a favor. Though she could never forgive his cruelty and in the following years reveled in his descent to laughable mediocrity, he had shown her, by casting her aside, the total worthlessness of romantic love.

Romantic love, if not entirely a fiction best relegated to movies and novels, was a waste of time and energy, and even more dangerously, a distraction the truly elite at their craft could not afford.

Scorned by her partner in her one adulterous fling from the true love of her life, Julia returned to the welcoming embrace of her violin. It took her in, forgave her transgressions, and made passionate love to her with the beauty they created together every day.

The performance at Symphony Hall the next night was even more transcendent. The thunderous applause and huzzahs washed over her. And when her boy toy arrived precisely on time and once again filled her with skin-tingling pleasure all over her body, she felt complete in a way she'd never felt before. Body and soul. Fulfilled in every way. Her music and her amazing boy toy. Euphoria flooded over her.

Until she realized with a start how she was showering him with kisses and he was responding in kind.

Not just sensual, erotic kisses. Kisses of the heart. Kisses of the soul.

Dangerous kisses.

Terrifying kisses.

Julia recoiled in sudden terror. Her eyes shot wide open. Her hands trembled with fear. Violently, she tore herself away from that emotional cliff. She couldn't allow herself to plunge over that edge. Could never allow it. Never again. It would be her ruination.

This coupling could only be to satisfy her, and the boy toy's, animalistic cravings. Nothing more. Never anything more. There could be no emotion.

Even though tearing herself away from it filled her heart with longing.

And so there were no more kisses of his soft lips. At least none to her own lips. Only to the other pleasurable parts of her body.

Especially *down there*. She shuddered as his kisses down there filled her carnal soul with euphoric bliss.

Sadness passed through Julia's mind in the knowledge that this evening's volcanic jubilation—the purest joy she'd ever known, first in the concert hall and then shockingly matched in the bedroom—would be hers for only this night, a bravura encore performance of the night before.

Never again.

Although...

Perhaps this bliss could endure for just one more achingly perfect evening.

Just one more!

Could she consider the forbidden fruit of a third night with this man? An unthinkable risk she'd never even contemplated. *A third night!*

But it would have the perfect symmetry of a Bach fugue. A third night of perfection at Boston's Symphony Hall capped off with the third night of sensual delight with this gorgeous man and his oh-so-pleasing, innocent smile, his stunning stamina, and his astonishing oral capabilities.

Fulfillment of body and soul. How could she deny it to herself? Just one more perfect night before leaving for Philadelphia, the next stop on the tour.

And so when they lay in each other's arms, their bodies tingling with pleasure but now totally spent, the wonderful boy toy's question had only one possible answer.

"Can I see you again?" he asked, his earnest, soft green eyes making Julia's heart melt.

There was only one possible answer.

"Tomorrow night," Julia said.

She was about to add that after that, they would never see each other again. The tour was moving on and she was already breaking all her rules about entanglements and all the dangers they represented. After Sunday night, their third night together, there could not be a fourth. It would not only be unwise to the point of recklessness, it was impossible. On to Philadelphia and the rest of the tour.

And the rest of her life. Without him.

The thought—the unshakable certainty of that reality—tore at her heart.

And so she could bear to say nothing more than the two words even though the rest of the truth filled her with a sense of overwhelming loss.

"Tomorrow night."

Chapter Six

Dressed in their trademark plaid red-and-white flannel shirts and black dress jeans, Slavko and the boys packed up their equipment and prepared to leave the Topsfield Fairgrounds for the last time. Never, ever, ever would the Pied Piper Polish Polka Dots return to this site of their most abject humiliation.

The smells of sausage, peppers, onions, cheeseburgers, and pizza still floated through the chilly fall air. Midway barkers could still be faintly heard, calling to passersby while bells clanged. And the rock and roll anthems of AC/DC—*music people loved, imagine that!*—pounded in the remote stretches of the fairgrounds where that relentless beat accompanied the screams of delighted passengers on the rides.

A few hours remained of the fair, but not for the Pied Piper Polish Polka Dots. Their final show was over. Stick a fork in them; they were done.

They'd endured many embarrassments over the years. No one needed to remind them that polka was at the opposite end of the spectrum—the far opposite end of the spectrum—from cool. Little more than a decade ago, the Grammy Awards removed the polka category because polka was no longer "representative of the musical landscape" and the award needed to be "relevant and responsive" to the music community. Not cool at all. But this humiliation topped them all.

Nothing even close.

The tented grassy area that could hold three hundred or more had remained painfully empty—not just sparsely attended but *empty*—except for those who'd popped in solely to ridicule. Worst of all had been when five teenaged boys popped in while Slavko, having set aside his tuba for the moment, and Happy Eddie were engaged in a fierce dueling accordion duet. Rock stars did that sort of thing with guitars all the time to roars of approval from stadium-sized adoring crowds, and some polka aficionados considered this accordion variation the height of many concerts.

But those five boys howled with laughter, showering the band with their derision to the point of stomping their feet and then rolling on the grass, their bodies shaking uncontrollably as if being electrocuted. Then to pour salt into the band's wounds, the boys, all white, hijacked "Cuckoo in the Clock Polka" and tried to turn it into a rap with obscene and racist lyrics. It had thrown off the usually unflappable Happy Eddie so badly that he'd stopped singing and playing the accordion, had just stared at the teenagers in horror as the rest of the band played on until Slavko waved them all into stunned silence.

Never again. They couldn't get out of here fast enough. And of course, there had been no financial bonus for impressive crowds.

It cut Slavko to the quick even worse than the other band members because as their leader he'd suggested they take the gig as a replacement for one in Pennsylvania that had cancelled. The fair had also suffered a cancellation due to a band breakup, so it had seemed a fortuitous coincidence. Instead, it had turned into a soul-crushing disaster. Both emotionally and finally because he'd only been able to get the gig by agreeing to a painfully low base rate with crowd-size bonuses that never came close to earning.

This was his fault, he supposed. The buck stopped with him. But there had been no alternatives. He'd taken what they could get, gambling that they could somehow attract crowds in this corner of the country that was as far from a polka stronghold as possible. He'd gambled and oh how they had lost. Nobody was saying it, but the disheartened looks on all their faces—even the almost-always-cheerful, ruddy-cheeked Happy Eddie—spoke volumes. They'd be heading back to their base in Wisconsin, with a dozen or so stops en route, with their tails between their legs.

"Sorry, boys," Slavko said to no one in particular as he slammed shut the red-and-white plaid trailer door, the three boys standing behind him. "Just got to put this behind us and move on. It's how this business works. Get knocked down. Get back up again."

He turned to face three stony glares. Silence hung in the chilly air for long seconds.

"And I'm afraid," he said, wincing at the need to say the next few words, "we need to hit the Costco a mile from here before we leave. Fill our bellies on the freebies."

It was among the most degrading things they'd had to subject themselves to of late. Eat a full meal by cycling through the massive store's free food samples. And if the samples weren't sufficient, or the dirty looks by the employees too humiliating to tolerate, then pay the buck-fifty for a large hot dog. It was an indignity that often seemed too great a burden to bear. It took paying dues for your art to new lows. But dead broke was dead broke.

No one moved.

Finally, Happy Eddie cleared his throat and looked away.

"Just tell us you didn't book this gig because of this girlfriend you've got in Boston," he said, his eyes abnormally cold and dark.

Slavko blinked. "Girlfriend? What girlfriend?"

He'd told no one of his secret meetings with the astonishing, nameless woman. He'd gone *somewhere*, of course, but had let them assume he'd just struck out. Not even hinted of it to Happy Eddie, his oldest friend in the world. Though Happy Eddie's prematurely white hair and beard made him look decades older than thirty-one, the two of them went all the way back to grammar school and told each other most everything, good and bad.

"The last two nights you've showered, shaved, and put on cologne, then disappeared into the night," Happy Eddie said. "Offered to drop us off at a bar or a strip joint—if we had any money for that sort of thing, that is, which we don't—but didn't offer for us to join you wherever you were going. And not to play detective or anything, but the mileage reading on the odometer says you've driven someplace like into Boston. And you said you needed the SUV again tonight.

"Now we don't care if it's a girlfriend, or for that matter, a boyfriend, although that would certainly surprise me, coming from you. But the last two nights you've been sprucing yourself up for something, like a goddamned Romeo, and since that first night you've been smiling all day long and humming like a teenager in love. I ain't seen you smitten like this since all those years ago with Norma Mae until she decided you weren't marriage material. It's like you're walking on air, at least until you get to these damned fairgrounds and that reality gives you a cold slap in the face.

"So if you set us up for this...this train wreck of a gig...this outright humiliation that paid us peanuts just because you've got a secret girlfriend up here, we got a right to know. And if we're so broke we've got to make another Costco run, how come you're out there wining and dining some lady friend night after night?"

<hr>

The endless fast food joints and gas stations along Route 1 passed slowly by as Slavko drove into Boston. Most of the fast food establishments on both sides were closed for the night, their neon lights turned off, leaving only McDonalds, Burger King, Kelly's Roast Beef, and the gas stations offering their wares until the three lanes on each side of the divided roadway merged into two and the roadside businesses disappeared entirely. The late-night traffic was light as Slavko crossed the Tobin Bridge into the city.

He felt euphoric at the opportunity to be with the amazing, nameless woman for a third night, but he also couldn't escape the despair of the band's crushing defeat at the fair. He'd been so naïve to think they could attract crowds to earn the extra dollars they so desperately needed.

He couldn't blame the boys for being mad at him. But Happy Eddie had been wrong about almost everything. There had been no girlfriend when Slavko had arranged for the Topsfield Fair gig. No surge of testosterone had fueled this blunder. There'd simply been no alternatives. He'd taken a long shot and it hadn't paid off.

From a purely selfish point of view—which wasn't his way of doing things *at all*, but that perspective couldn't be denied—this train wreck, to use Happy Eddie's phrase for it, had allowed Slavko two magical nights with this amazing woman. This Chinese goddess of beauty and sensuality and something more he couldn't define but couldn't get enough of. With a third meeting less than an hour away.

He hadn't been wining and dining her, as Happy Eddie had insinuated, spending lavishly while everyone else remained penniless, holed up in their Motel 6 room. His wallet was as empty as theirs. He hadn't even had to pay half of the hotel bill. Her original instructions on the DiscreetPartnerForYou app had been that she would pay the bill, no questions asked, and would notify him of the location on the day of their meeting.

Slavko pushed the band's unhappiness from his mind. There was nothing he could do about that right now. Instead, he considered the upcoming week. The band had to move on to Schenectady, New York, just outside of Albany. There was no changing that. Those tour dates were rock solid, which was a good thing for the band. It couldn't withstand another cancellation.

Even so, Slavko would be tempted to sell his soul to the Devil for a fourth night with his magical, nameless woman. Even if that fourth night couldn't be until a month or two or three from now. Somehow, he'd have to see her again. Tonight could not be the end.

Her petite beauty was breathtaking, even when masked by the obvious disguises: the rust-colored wig, the fake eyeglasses more befitting a librarian, and the excess of makeup, especially the bright red lipstick. Her exuberant sexuality was thrilling, like nothing he'd ever experienced before. And the mystery of her identity—she wouldn't divulge so much as a hint to even her first name—added even further to her allure.

But there was something more.

Slavko didn't know what it was, but he'd fallen head over heels for her that first night. That first night of incomparable sexual bliss, ending in loving kisses—*the birth of something lasting?*—until she'd abruptly cut them off and dismissed him.

He'd fallen even harder for her the next night when the kisses became even more long and loving. Kisses *she* initiated! She'd given every indication that she was falling for him as hard as he was falling for her—if such a thing were even possible—and what had been mere, mind-blowing, astonishing sex became *making love*. Their hearts and souls becoming one.

At least that's what he thought. Only to have her suddenly pull back from all emotion and throw up a brick wall. Allowing only sexual bliss. Physically amazing. But soulless.

He would break through that wall tonight. Even if this was his last night in Boston. Even if it would be next to impossible to see her again. He *had* to see her again.

Love would find a way.

Slavko blinked.

Love.

He'd actually thought that word. *Love.* Because he felt it. What had started as lust, a lonely satisfying of mutual desires, had become love. Which certainly seemed backwards. He'd always believed in falling in love first and then moving on to sex, or more accurately, making love.

But who was he to question how fate had brought him together with this goddess? Backward? Forward? Who cared? The end result was unquestionably love.

Love.

And somehow, Slavko had no idea exactly how, he would keep this amazing love alive even as the two of them inevitably separated.

Slavko and the goddess lay on the hotel room bed, exhausted, their sweat intermingling. More than satisfied. Fulfilled. Euphoric.

Even though he was spent, drained dry, even inch of his skin still tingled. He stroked the woman's arm. Then her hip. He smelled the strawberry scent of her hair and the lavender scent of her neck.

He kissed her sweet lips. Long and lovingly. They tasted faintly of wintergreen. Then her neck. She groaned softly.

He loved this woman. Could not let this night be their last together.

"I know this isn't how it's supposed to work," Slavko whispered in her ear, wrapping his arms around her. "But can you please tell me something about yourself?"

Slavko felt her stiffen in his arms.

"I'll go first," he added quickly. "I'll tell you anything. I'll happily tell you my entire life story. I'm sorry if that's breaking the rules, but I just can't get enough of you. Not just sexually, although that of course has been mind-boggling. I just..."

The word "love" word almost spilled out. It's what he felt and he knew she felt *something*, too. But there were those other times when he felt them becoming so very close, intimate in more than just a sexual way, only to have her—this amazing goddess—pull away from him. Go distant. And now she was stiffening at his words like a frozen slab of ice.

No, "love" was not the right thing to say even though he felt it. Felt it after only three nights, which was inconceivable. But what an amazing three nights! And in truth, he'd been thunderstruck the moment he first saw her. She'd taken his breath away.

Had that been love at first sight? If it wasn't, he knew one thing for sure. He was now head over heels, ass over teakettle, crazy in love with her. Totally smitten.

And this was not a case of the head between his legs doing the thinking. This was his heart doing the thinking, doing the talking. Impossible after just three nights, but his heart was hers. Even though he didn't even know her name!

"My name is Slavko," he said. "I'll tell you anything."

"Stop!" the goddess said, pulling away entirely and jumping out of the bed, her rust-colored wig noticeably askew.

The look of sheer terror in her eyes broke Slavko's heart. She stepped slowly away from him as if he were a serial killer wielding a gun or knife.

"I'm sorry," he said, reaching out a hand and beckoning her back. "I've said the wrong thing. I'm sorry. I'll never speak again. Not another word. Not for the rest of my life. As long as I can be with you." And then the words spilled out even though he tried to hold them in. "I can't get enough of you."

"Stop it!" she almost screeched.

It felt like a cold slap in the face. He fell silent—*like I should have been all along*—and stared at the goddess. She held a hand to her mouth. She was almost trembling.

"I'm so sorry!" Slavko said. "I meant no harm!"

"Please go," she said in barely more than a whisper.

"Okay," Slavko said, rolling off the bed and grabbing his shorts and slacks off the floor. "Just tell me we can meet again. I don't care if you ever tell me your name or anything about yourself. Just let me make you happy. Tell me we can meet again."

Slavko had no idea how that could happen. He and the rest of the band would be leaving in the morning. And would never, ever, ever return to Boston.

But Slavko didn't care. He had to see this woman again.

And again. And again.

He'd have to find a way.

"No, we can never meet again," the woman said, tears pooling in her soft eyes. She shook her head. "It's impossible. I leave Boston tomorrow."

Slavko blinked in surprise. "So do I!"

The woman stared wide-eyed at him. "Then why did you ask about meeting again?"

"Because I have to see you again! I love you!"

Slavko's eyes widened, horrified at his words. Words of absolute truth. But the wrong words to have blurted out.

The goddess stared back at him in even greater horror.

"No! No! No!" she said. "You can't say that! You can't mean that! Please leave!"

"I'm sorry!" Slavko said, fumbling hopelessly for the right words. "Just give me—"

"Get out!" the goddess yelled, pointing at the door, tears streaming down her face.

Feeling like a whipped dog, Slavko dressed as fast as he could and stumbled out the door.

Chapter Seven

J ulia cried all night.

Back in her upscale Beacon Hill condo, she lay tormented in her king-size mahogany bed that felt so very, very empty, as if it were a vast blue ocean that stretched to the horizon in all directions unblemished except for a single tiny, yellow life raft bobbing in the waves with her inside. Her obscenely expensive mattress that was supposed to provide maximum comfort for her tiny figure offered no comfort at all as she tossed and turned. Her custom pillow, contoured to fit the curve of her neck, vulnerable to debilitating nerve and muscle pain that ended many violinists' careers, soothed none of the pain in Julia's heart. It was wet on both sides with her tears.

Through bleary eyes, she stared at the digital clock resting on the mahogany nightstand. Its red numbers refused to change in anything more than the slowest of slow motions.

3:14.

3:14.

3:14.

3:14.

3:14.

3:15.

3:15.

3:15.

3:15.

3:15.

No matter what she did, Julia couldn't get that man—he'd called himself Slavko, such a unique, unforgettable name for such unique, unforgettable man—out of her mind. Especially the crestfallen, puppy-dog look when in a panic she'd ordered him out of the hotel room.

Slavko.

Why had he ruined everything? Asking her to tell him something, anything, about herself. Offering to tell her his entire life story. Told her his name.

Slavko.

And then, after saying he couldn't get enough of her, he'd used the L word!

"I have to see you again!" he'd said. "I love you!"

Love.

Of course, she'd panicked. Of course, she'd thrown him out. Of course, she'd had no choice.

He was supposed to be nothing more than an innocent boy toy. One who serviced her every desire. A requirement he'd fulfilled with boy-toy enthusiasm, stunning stamina, and mind-boggling expertise.

Especially when he moved his mouth *down there* and used his lips and tongue to drive her wild like no man had ever done before. And had allowed her—had encouraged her!—to sit on his face and press down on those lips and tongue, cutting off his oxygen for what felt like a blissful eternity while the orgasms rolled over her and shook her body.

The very memory sparked a tingle of pleasure and wetness between her legs.

Could she be blamed for having invited him back a second night, breaking her most sacred rule of passion? How could she not have indulged herself with such pleasure a second time? And then a third?

If only there could be a fourth and a fifth. A sixth and a seventh. If only there could be no end to her time with him. Sharing not only orgasmic pleasure but those sweet, loving kisses. Holding each other. Smiles of not just contentment but happiness and pure joy. Feeling a special warmth in her heart she'd never felt before.

If only he could be here right now.

But such thoughts were madness. She would be leaving for Philadelphia later today with concerts there on Friday, Saturday, and Sunday. And he, Slavko, had said that he would be leaving Boston, too.

So it was settled.

Unless he, too, was going to Philadelphia.

But that wouldn't merely be the unlikeliest of coincidences. It was also out of the question.

He'd used the L word. And there was no going back from that.

Her fault, of course. If she hadn't broken her one-night-only rule, they both wouldn't be in this mess. Slavko would have merely entered her Boy Toy Hall of Fame as the single most orally skilled lover of all time.

One and done. The way it was supposed to be.

Instead, the kisses of purest carnal desire had become kisses loaded with explosive emotion. Kisses of those soft lips of his that tasted of some sort of mint. Long, lingering kisses as he lovingly caressed her body and she slid her fingertips across his powerful, barrel-shaped chest and through his thick, wavy hair.

Sweet kisses filled with passion. But sweet, loving kisses.

She couldn't get enough of them. And neither had he.

Sure enough—what the hell had been wrong with her?—their animalistic rutting, two lonely souls fulfilling their most basic desires, had become lovemaking.

Lovemaking! Undeniably lovemaking!

The L word!

She wouldn't have uttered the word herself. She had permanently removed it from her vocabulary.

But she had felt it. Hadn't she? That longing in her heart for this man called Slavko. As she'd waited for him in that hotel room, she'd wanted no other boy toy. She wanted him and him alone.

Slavko, the greatest boy toy of all time, had relinquished that title.

He had become her lover.

Julia wanted to scream in frustration. What was wrong with her? Hadn't she learned her lesson with Xiangyu? Romance and her career did not mix. *Could not* coexist. And she'd be damned if now that she'd reached the pinnacle of her profession she'd throw it all away.

For nothing more than a mere man.

One who would discard her like a used napkin just as Xiangyu had done. One who would pull her down from her hard-earned pinnacle and then view her with nothing more than disdain.

Never again. She owed herself that much.

3:19.

3:19.

3:19.

Besides, Julia told herself, romantic love was a fiction. It didn't even exist. Nonsense reserved for movies, novels, and sappy Hallmark cards.

She'd told herself that countless times since Xiangyu's treachery. No such thing as love. She'd believed it with all of her heart.

Even so, Julia couldn't silence the question she kept asking herself.

What was this longing she felt in her heart? If love was a fiction, then what was this longing?

A longing for Slavko and Slavko alone.

Chapter Eight

It felt like a funeral inside the Ford Explorer. The heated air was heavy and thick. It smelled of Costco hot dogs slathered in mustard, robotically consumed. Slavko, sitting shotgun, knew he was powerless to change the mood.

Happy Eddie looked none too happy behind the steering wheel. He always kept his eyes locked on the road, and Route 95's heavy traffic gave him even more reason to focus his attention. But he hadn't given Slavko even the slightest glance since backing the SUV and trailer out of its Motel 6 parking space, driving the band to Costco for all the free samples they could shovel down before grabbing hot dogs to go, then taking off for Route 95 and the Mass Pike.

Not even a glance.

Happy Eddie just stared straight ahead, lips pursed. He would always feature the Santa Claus–like beard and beefy, ruddy cheeks that people noticed first when he was, as was almost always the case, happy. But at times like this, there was no jolly laughter in Happy Eddie's brooding, dark eyes. Now, he was pissed-off Santa. Or worse. His eyes were more like a serial killer's than St. Nick's.

When the country music sounding from the radio gave way to more and more frequent bursts of harsh static, Happy Eddie, who as the driver got to choose the music, stabbed one preset after another with his index finger. Stabbed hard enough to either break the black plastic or his finger. Or both.

Behind them, Junior and Silent Wally sat in the rear seats, sullen and silent, their eyes boring holes into the back of Slavko's skull, at least until Junior finally began to snore.

Persona non grata.

That's how Slavko felt, but there was nothing he could do about it. With his own heart crushed by his beautiful Chinese goddess, he couldn't lift his own spirits out of the darkest depths, much less anyone else's.

He closed his eyes and tried once again to sleep, knowing he had no chance in the suddenly claustrophobic confines. His legs felt cramped. Not exactly pinned up against his chest, but with Silent Wally and his long, spindly legs behind him, Slavko couldn't come close to stretching his own legs out, and time after time felt Silent Wally's knobby knees poking into the back of the seat. Slavko shook his head in frustration. He licked his dry lips but couldn't rid his mouth of the taste of the Costco samples and hot dogs, or the remnants of the free Motel 6 coffee he'd just finished off, cold and unsatisfying. His stomach rumbled in protest at their poor man's meal.

He rested his head against the cool side window. As if on cue, they once again hit a bump in the road that jerked his head straight up, then smacked it back down against the glass. Probably a reflection of imperfections in the road. Or possibly, a driver with a bad attitude.

Happy Eddie's phone, mounted in a black plastic holder on the Explorer's black dashboard, indicated the ride to their destination in upstate New York would take almost another three hours.

It would feel more like three days. Maybe even thirty.

Slavko let his mind wander back to last night's bliss. The sensual pleasures, of course. They could not be denied. Especially the moans and gasps of ecstasy coming from his lover's lips. There was nothing better than giving her pleasure.

But somehow her soft, loving kisses had been even more fulfilling. Both while his hands caressed every curve of her body and also when he held her so very tight, never wanting to let her go. The wintergreen taste on her lips. The smell of strawberries in her hair, or perhaps in that flagrantly fake rust-haired wig.

Pure bliss. Until it all came crashing down. Heartbreakingly so.

And now this.

From the penthouse to the outhouse.

Slavko turned in his seat, his back to the window, and tried to blank his mind. Sleep. He desperately needed sleep, if for no other reason than to escape the mental outhouse he now found himself in.

Happy Eddie turned the radio off and coughed loudly. The sound of a steel guitar gave way to the outside hum of tires on asphalt. And then an angry honk of a horn.

Slavko opened his eyes.

"I hope she was worth it, Romeo," Happy Eddie said, still staring straight ahead.

The words felt like a hard slap on the face. As they'd been intended.

Silence hung heavy in the air.

Slavko bit back a reply that yes, the goddess had very much been worth it. Every wonderful second with her had been priceless. Even if she had, in the end, broken his heart. Pushed him out the door without the chance of ever seeing her again.

Which would have been next to impossible anyway.

Impossible, short of leaving the band he'd sacrificed everything to form and then nurture into what amounted to fame in the tiny world of polka. Dammit, he'd sacrificed everything for this band. And for what?

At times like this, with those band mates turning against him—even Happy Eddie, his oldest friend in the world—Slavko had to question those sacrifices. Had it all been a waste?

Perhaps his parents and Norma Mae had been right after all. Maybe this was a fool's pursuit.

Norma Mae. Sweet Norma Mae. He'd even sacrificed her at this damned silly altar of polka and the tuba. Calling it "his art" when it seemed as though almost every last human being under the age of ninety considered it worthy of only ridicule.

For that fool's dream, he'd sacrificed Norma Mae, her hair the color of shucked corn and her shoulders and arms strong from milking cows since she was barely ten. They'd been high school sweethearts. She was a farmer's daughter. He was a farmer's son. Everyone assumed they would marry and, of course, become farmers themselves and spawn a half dozen babies who would grow up and in turn, help in the fields, milk the cows, and even spread the manure.

It was inevitable.

Until the night of The Talk.

They'd been sitting on the wooden bench on the porch outside her parents' house, a full moon high in the sky and an owl hooting in the distance, holding hands, bundled up against the brisk autumn wind, using it as an excuse to snuggle closer.

"We need to talk about us," Norma Mae said, her voice as firm as her grip on his hand.

Slavko felt his eyes widen for a brief moment. He nodded. "Okay."

"We'll be graduating high school in half a year and neither of us plans to go to college," Norma Mae said. "We ain't going nowhere, we're both staying right here. At least, that's what seems to be the plan, even though you never talk about it. So I need to know where we stand. Where I stand."

Slavko gulped.

"Well, I've been thinking a lot about that lately," he said.

Norma Mae smiled sweetly. Hopefully.

Slavko looked away. He tried to summon the courage to say what he'd been afraid to tell his parents. Crazy talk. He knew they'd look at him like he was a fool. And tell him to get his silly ideas out of his head. This was the real world, not some fantasyland like in the movies where everyone got to do exactly what they wished.

He hoped Norma Mae would understand. She was a compassionate, loving soul. Accepting him for what he was.

He took a deep breath.

"It seems like everyone expects me to just be like my pa," Slavko said. He felt Norma Mae stiffen beside him, but continued on. There was no stopping now. "As the only son, I'd eventually take over the farm, especially after my sisters got married. But I'm not sure that's what I want."

Norma Mae looked at him, a look of confusion covering her face. "What *do* you want?"

Slavko took another deep breath.

"Well, you know how I love music," he said. "And I'm pretty good at it. Both the tuba and accordion, and I can sing okay, too. But especially the tuba. When Happy Eddie and I play at the fair each year along with whoever else we can rustle up, we're as good as anyone else. Better, even."

Slavko waited, letting his words sink in while summoning the courage to speak what came next.

"You can still keep doing all of that," Norma Mae said, squinting her brown eyes ever so slightly as if to see him better. "Play your tuba and accordion with Happy Eddie every Friday and Saturday night, if you want, and still work the farm. No one would deny you that, least of all me. I love you."

She squeezed his hand to emphasize those last three words.

Slavko swallowed hard. He loved her, too, but her words were making this harder.

"I want to play my music more than that," he said. "Not just on Friday and Saturday nights. Not just here in town in front of the same few people every weekend. I want to play my music all the time. Everywhere. And I can't do that if I'm working the farm. Not if I'm carrying my weight. And when my pa can't work it anymore and it's all on my shoulders, then I'll be lucky if I can even manage Friday and Saturday nights in town."

"So what are you saying?" Norma Mae asked, her voice tinged with fear.

Slavko once again took a deep breath.

"I don't want to be a farmer. I want to be a musician."

Silence filled the chilly air.

"A *professional* musician?" Norma Mae asked in obvious disbelief.

"Yes," Slavko said. "I want to try, at least."

"A professional *polka* musician?"

"Yes!"

"Does such a thing even exist?" Norma Mae asked, her disbelief turning into what felt like disdain.

"It won't be easy," Slavko conceded. "For a time, maybe even a long time, I'll need to work some other job to make ends meet. I certainly won't just be sitting around the house. You know me. I'm willing to work as hard as it takes. But it'll have to be a job with the flexibility to travel to other state fairs as often as possible. To go on tours."

"Travel? Tours? How often? How long would you be gone?" Norma Mae asked.

"As long as it takes," Slavko said. "I suppose for quite some time during a tour. Lots of musicians are on the road for most of the year."

Norma Mae's eyes all but popped out. "Most of the year?"

Slavko could only nod.

"What kind of life is that?" she asked, incredulous. "Off gallivanting here, there, and everywhere. Groupies throwing themselves at you—"

"I'm sure there aren't—"

"And I'm supposed to sit here at home, patiently waiting for *The Famous Musician*"—she practically spit the term out—"who is too good to be a simple, old farmer like everyone else he grew up with. No, he's too good for that! I'm supposed to wait for him to return home from his *worldwide polka tour*"—more words spat out in derision—"and welcome him with open arms and wonder how many strange women he's been with during that long, lonely time without me!"

"It wouldn't be like that!" Slavko protested. "I would never cheat—"

"That may be the life you want, but I'll have no part of it," Norma Mae said. "You can chase your foolish pipe dreams all you want, and good luck to you. But I'll have no part of it. I just wish you'd told me all of this before we ever started going out."

"I didn't know—"

"Before I ever fell in love with you," she said, her voice choking.

"I'm sorry. I—"

"I wish I'd never, ever met you!"

Norma Mae stood, tears pooling in her brown eyes. She yanked off the promise ring Slavko had given her at the Harvest Dance a year ago, almost as soon as they'd begun dating. He'd had no money, so it was a simple, cheap silver thing with two hearts on it, barely better than a plastic ring found in a Cracker Jack box, but it meant something. They would date only each other. No one else.

And yes, it held the promise of possibly even more.

Norma Mae slapped the ring into his palm. Fury filled her tear-filled eyes.

"Get out of my sight!" she said, seething. "I never want to see you again! And good luck on your goddamned tour!"

It was the first time Slavko had ever heard her swear. The first time she'd ever even raised her voice like that at him. The first time he'd seen those brown eyes filled with anything but love for him.

Eyes now filled with pain. But even more than that.

Hatred.

Hatred for what he had done to her even though he hadn't known the half of this—the extent of his dreams and how much he'd be willing to sacrifice to achieve them—until only very recently. And had truly believed them himself only just now when he'd summoned the courage to speak them aloud.

***

"Cat got your tongue, Romeo?"

Happy Eddie's angry voice jerked Slavko back from his thoughts. Back from losing Norma Mae for...

... for *this*.

"Seems like all you're thinking about is this piece of tail of yours," Happy Eddie continued, a Rottweiler now with raw meat in its jaws, dripping blood. "And I ain't the only one who feels that way." He jerked a thumb toward the back seat. "These guys can't say it, so I've got to. If you don't get your head screwed on straight and stick to business instead of carousing with the ladies, it's gonna be the end of the Polka Dots."

Slavko tried to remember the original question. It took a few long, torturous moments before it came to him.

I hope she was worth it, Romeo.

Not even a question. Just a snide accusation. More than snide. Angry. Then insulting the way he'd been running the band. Spearheading what wouldn't be a near mutiny like last time when he announced the temporary pay cuts. This time would be an all-out mutiny.

Coming from his best friend. *Et tu Brute?*

Slavko turned in his seat, the belt tightening around his broad shoulders and waist, so he could stare at each of them in turn. Then back to Happy Eddie.

Something snapped.

Slavko had no idea if it was the old memory flashing through his mind of losing Norma Mae for this miserable life on the road. *For nothing!* Or losing the astonishing Chinese goddess before he ever really, truthfully had her. *But dammit, there had been something, he was sure of it, there was something!* Or the humiliations and all the derision showered upon them at the Topsfield Fair and all the other misguided venues they'd chosen—*he'd* chosen! Or that the point man for this mutiny was Happy Eddie himself, Slavko's oldest friend in the world.

Or all of the above.

But something snapped with an almost audible *crack*.

"*Who the hell do you guys think you are?*" Slavko yelled.

All three recoiled, shrinking away from him, even Happy Eddie who momentarily lost his focus on the road.

"If any of you three know-it-alls think you can do a better job leading this band," Slavko continued at maximum decibels, "then be my *bleeping* guest! And I'll be happy to second-guess you into oblivion, too!" Slavko glared for long seconds. "Any one of you clowns dumb enough to volunteer?"

The silence screamed in Slavko's ears.

"It's just—" Happy Eddie finally began.

"*It's just what?*" Slavko shouted.

No one said anything for what felt like hours. Happy Eddie stared straight ahead, eyes slightly widened. Junior and Silent Wally leaned as far back in their seats as possible in an apparent futile attempt to get away from the madman in their midst.

Finally, whatever had snapped inside Slavko popped back into place.

Instantly, he felt bad. What had he done now?

Many, if not most or even all, bands suffered through arguments like this. It was a casualty of the road. Too many bodies cooped up in too small a space for too many hours. Too many soul-crushing disappointments and too few successes. Too many jealousies. Too many frayed nerves. It became inevitable. Harsh words got spoken and at decibels approaching the roar of an aircraft taking off.

Part of the life.

But that wasn't how Slavko did things. If one of the boys sniped at another, it was his job to put out the fire before it engulfed them all. Instead, this time he'd escalated the confrontation. Poured gasoline on the flames. Turned some second-guessing—infuriating, but probably understandable in a calmer light—into World War III.

Slavko felt like crap.

"Sorry, man," he said to Happy Eddie.

His old, Santa Claus–like friend gave a single curt nod.

Slavko turned toward the back seat. "Same to you guys, too."

Silent Wally and Junior nodded in unison but warily.

Slavko pointed to Happy Eddie. "You were saying."

"Forget it," Happy Eddie said.

"No, tell me." Slavko said. "We need to make this right. Not let it fester."

"You sure?"

"Yes, you were saying, 'It's only' and then I bit your head off," Slavko said. In a peacemaking gesture, Slavko forced a grin and corrected his words, "I bit your *ugly* head off."

The tightest of grins formed on the corners of Happy Eddie's mouth, camouflaged by his Santa Claus beard. "I bet you say that to all the boys."

"Only to your *three* ugly mugs," Slavko said with the best smile he could muster, swinging his focus from Happy Eddie to Junior to Silent Wally and back again.

Slavko felt the tension plummet.

"Let's hear it," he said.

"What I was saying," Happy Eddie began, "is that it was tough for the rest of us to be miserable, getting our teeth kicked in for this entire gig while you were walking around—except for during the performances themselves—as if nothing was wrong. As if you didn't care that we're a ship going down in shark-infested waters. Acting like you were the king of the world with Lady Gaga for his queen. And who gives a shit about your loyal subjects. Rubbing our noses in it, for crying out loud."

"I—"

"Let me finish," Happy Eddie insisted, his eyes maintaining their laser beam focus on the road. "Of course, you weren't *trying* to rub our noses in it, and of course, we were glad that you were happy. But for crying out loud, you should have spent some time around yourself these last few days. You say to us, 'Girlfriend? What girlfriend?' But it's been like you're walking in the clouds. Dancing on air. Humming one love song after another, not even realizing you're doing it, with a huge, shit-eating grin on your face. Going out at night all spruced up and smelling of cologne, a goddamned Romeo, and coming back smelling of perfume and acting like your dick has died and gone to Heaven. Actually, not just your dick. All of you. Jesus, you've been like a Disney movie.

"So it feels like you're rubbing our noses in it, spending money chasing tail. Money that we sure as shit don't have, especially after you cut our pay. We're staying at a Motel 6 just a mile away from a strip joint called the Golden Banana, and we can't even afford the cover charge. Our idea of fine dining is eating all the free samples at Costco we can stuff into our guts and then grab hot dogs to go. We're all dead broke and you claim that you are, too, but then you're out there partying all night. You say you can't get us any extra paying gigs, but you're spending all your extra time with this woman. Having a grand time while the band swirls down the crapper.

"We go back a long way, Slavko, but it's hard to believe you suddenly discovered this woman of your dreams the first day we got here. Hard to believe you had no idea she was here when you booked this Gig From Hell. She just fell out of the sky into your lap and it was True Love and Great Sex at first sight. And hard as hell to believe you're as focused as you need to be to save this band.

"Now I've known you almost all my entire life," Happy Eddie continued. "If you say you're doing everything you can to replace our cancellations and pick up extra gigs, and you say this woman had nothing to do with you signing us up for last damned gig that paid us peanuts, then I'll have to believe you. But it's a tough story you're selling, and right now, your audience is in a damned cranky mood."

Slavko nodded for the longest time, trying to figure out what to say.

"Okay, I hear you," he said, still fumbling for words. "Not that my love life is anyone else's business, but I hear you. This one time makes sense. But never again. I don't ask you guys about your love lives and you don't ask about mine. Here's the God's honest truth, and after this I don't want to hear another word about it."

Slavko waited until they all nodded.

"Yes, I did find someone purely by chance and experienced three amazing nights with her," he said. "I'll say nothing more about her cause it's nobody's business but mine, but I didn't meet her until Friday night and I certainly didn't schedule that damned Topsfield Fair appearance around someone I'd never met until we were already here. I would never do that to you guys. And believe it or not, I'm as broke as all three of you. That's no BS. I haven't paid a damned cent for anything other than the gas these last three nights."

Stunned silence fell.

"Yeah, right," Junior said from the diagonally opposite back seat, snorting in disbelief. "Like we're supposed to believe that?"

Slavko leaned as close to Junior as his seat belt allowed. His eyes narrowed. "If you don't believe every word I'm saying, you're free to leave. We'll find the nearest bus home for you and I'll somehow find a way to pay for the ticket."

Silence again fell like a shroud.

"Junior, if the man says it, I believe it," Happy Eddie said. "Slavko don't lie."

Junior gulped and shrugged his shoulders. "Whatever you say."

Slavko eyed the other three men, one by one.

"As for not working hard enough to line up gigs," Slavko said, trying to hold back his rising anger, "you guys should know better than that. You hear me on the phone all day long. I shouldn't have to tell you this ain't polka country. Ain't much polka country anywhere these days, but this sure ain't it. And around midnight into the wee hours when I've been with my lady friend, that ain't the time I can be calling for gigs. That cheap shot is out of line and I deserve an apology."

Mumbled indecipherable words came from the back seat. Behind the steering wheel, Happy Eddie gave a quick nod and said, "Sorry. Never should have questioned you. My bad."

"For the record," Slavko added with a sinking heart, "I'll never see the woman again. She was something else, but it just can't happen. So I'll be as miserable as you three stooges. In fact, maybe even more miserable."

Miles passed in awkward silence before Happy Eddie thought to turn the radio back on. No one spoke even as one exit off the highway passed after another.

Chapter Nine

Sunlight streamed through the floor-to-ceiling glass wall, its drapes pulled back to offer the perfect mid-morning vista of the Philadelphia skyline from the luxurious penthouse-level hotel suite. Julia sat at the room's fifteen-foot-wide polished oak desk, the king-size bed behind her. She tapped her foot on the thick, blue-gray rug and on the same beat, drummed her pen idly on a hotel memo pad. Images flickered on the large-screen TV to her right. She ignored them and kept the audio on mute. Nothing on the TV or for that matter, the view of the skyline, interested her.

She sipped her steaming hot coffee, enjoying its dark roast richness not at all. On the wall to the left, the framed print of van Gogh's *Starry Night* felt as cloying in a pretentious sort of way as a Velvet Elvis. The lemon smell on the wooden furnishings made her nose want to itch.

This miserable afternoon had followed an equally miserable morning. Strangely inappropriate for what should be a high moment of her life. Living the dream. The world wasn't just her oyster. She already held handfuls of its pearls.

Even so, Philadelphia felt hollow and empty.

Not the city itself. The city was as vibrant as ever. Usually one of Julia's favorites. From the concert venue to the discerning audiences to the bustling city's level of excitement. Excited talk in the elevators about their sports teams: the Eagles, Sixers, and Flyers with their seasons underway and the Phillies considering trade options during their offseason. Excited and unabashedly proud of their Philly cheesesteak sandwiches, which were not at all to Julia's taste though she'd always been smart enough to keep that unpopular sentiment to herself. And yes, the city's arts community was also excited about Julia's stop there on her worldwide tour. Wall-to-wall interviews today, her preferred Media Day in her carefully scripted schedule. Sold-out shows on Friday, Saturday, and Sunday.

More excitement than she could muster herself right now. On Friday when she stood on stage with the violin in her hands, the thrill would return. Julia had no doubt of that. She would make musical love to that instrument as she always did.

La Petite Rockette would return.

But right now, she felt only hollow and empty. And she knew the problem was not with the city. It was with her.

She had immersed herself in all the day's usual pre-concert tasks. Interviews with two newspapers, two radio stations, and a TV show, all of which had gone well as she'd turned on a bright smile that she hadn't felt inside. After dinner this evening with several notable supporters of the orchestra, she would finally get to her uninterrupted hours of private practice that seemed as essential to everyday life as breathing. Perhaps her joy would return then, but she had her doubts.

She'd proceeded through the day with metronomic regularity. And that was the problem. All metronome and no passion. Hollow and empty of passion, outside of the fake smiles for the interviews. Understandable if she were months into the tour with no end in sight, the succession of hotel suites and restaurants blurring together, the maddening repetition of the same interview questions over and over to the point where she could predict the next question before even its first word was uttered.

But this wasn't months into the tour. This was only the second stop on a tour that would last almost a year. She should not be feeling emotionally drained at this point. Her tank should still be full, if not overflowing.

She sipped more of the coffee, no longer piping hot. Trending toward lukewarm. Which was how she felt inside.

Lukewarm. Hollow and empty of passion.

Slavko.

Damn that name! Damn that man!

He kept popping unbidden into her head. She'd tried to push all thoughts of him out of her mind ever since that final night of theirs together in Boston, and hoped she'd cried sufficient tears to flush him out of her system. Leave all memories of him behind in Boston. Be rid of him forever.

A new city. A new challenge. And if she needed to blow off steam again, a new man. This time, for one night only. Never a second night ever again. And for nothing more than hedonistic pleasure.

But she didn't want a new man. Not for any nights. Not for any sort of pleasure. Not for anything.

She wanted Slavko. No one else. Even if the fool had used the L word.

Dammit, his memory had followed her here to Philadelphia and was haunting her every step. That sweet man. With his barrel chest and innocent smile and good God almighty, those magical lips and tongue. And unfortunately, a magical heart intertwined with hers.

She couldn't get rid of him. Slavko and his damned L word hung darkly over her waking hours like a shroud.

She couldn't be happy without him.

Couldn't be happy without him?

Had she actually thought that? Yes, she had. Because it was true! Horribly and ominously true.

Slavko. She wanted to see him again. Simply *had* to see him again.

Not just because of his magical lips and tongue, though she certainly wouldn't deny herself that pleasure. She wanted all of Slavko. To hold him and kiss him and feel his kisses and his caresses.

To shower him with love. Make sweet, soulful love to that beautiful man.

But she couldn't!

It would be the most self-destructive thing ever!

Hadn't she learned her lesson with Xiangyu? She thought she had, but clearly she hadn't. And now she was paying the price. She was like Eve in the Garden of Eden, desiring the one thing forbidden to her. And if she insisted on continuing this obsession with Slavko, it would lead to her destruction just as it had with Xiangyu.

Banishment from her musical Garden of Eden.

Julia drew in a deep breath and shuddered. She looked down at the once-blank memo pad and realized she'd subconsciously scribbled Slavko's name over and over from the top of the page to the bottom, crossing it out each time and then writing it back in one line lower.

In her other hand, she held her phone. With the DiscreetPartner-ForYou app already visible and ready to open. With one click, she could check to see if Slavko had sent her a message. Or she could send him one herself.

The hand holding her phone trembled. Julia licked her dry lips.

One click.

What could it hurt?

Slavko. Those sweet green eyes. That innocent smile. And that not-so-innocent mouth and lips. Those wonderfully naughty mouth and lips.

Slavko. Slavko. Slavko.

Julia swallowed hard. She wanted him more than anything. More than anything in the world.

More than anything except her music.

Her music. What she'd devoted her life to do.

She couldn't allow herself to be destroyed again. Not now. Not ever.

Slavko was her Serpent in the Garden. A sweet serpent. At least, a *seemingly* sweet serpent. But a Serpent whispering that she could have it all. A Serpent who would cause her ruination. Get her expelled from her musical Garden of Eden.

Julia turned off her phone, set it down, then tore the sheet with Slavko's crossed-out names from the memo pad. She crumpled it into a ball and hurled it into the trash bucket beneath the desk.

She scribbled one line on a fresh sheet on the memo pad.

Slavko is the Serpent!

Chapter Ten

The twang of country music reverberated from the dashboard speakers. Warm, heavy air poured from the heating vents. In the middle lane up ahead, a car horn blared. Tires hummed on the Mass Pike asphalt. Slavko shifted in his passenger-side seat, unable to get comfortable. The stale smell of hot dogs long since consumed still lingered, perhaps from the balled-up wrappers stuffed in a paper bag tucked beneath his seat. The cloying odor tempted him to roll down the windows and get some fresh, clean air, but he resisted the temptation. The cold air would blow in hard on Junior and Silent Wally in the back seat. With the tensions between him and the boys finally settling down, Slavko was loathe to doing anything to break the peace.

Even though he never wanted to eat another hot dog for as long as he lived.

Slavko settled back in his seat and closed his eyes. He drew in a deep breath and was on the verge of drifting off to sleep when a loud squealing and ominous clanking noise erupted from the rear undercarriage.

Slavko sat bolt upright, eyes wide open.

No. Not now.

He looked over at Happy Eddie, who appeared every bit as alarmed, his knuckles white as he held the steering wheel in a death grip. He glanced in the rear view and side mirrors, then guided the Explorer as it clattered, clanked, and squealed its way over into the breakdown lane.

They slowed until a loud snap rang out. The SUV lurched forward and then ground to a shuddering halt.

Panic flooded through Slavko. This could not be coming at a worse time. Fate was kicking them in the head when they were already down and almost comatose.

Slavko shook his head and climbed out of the car. The others also spilled out as the three lanes of traffic zoomed by. He clenched his eyes shut for a brief moment, feeling as though he'd been kicked in the gut. This was worse than "when it rains, it pours." Far worse. This was "when it rains, it's a tornado and it's going to rip your house from its foundation, tear it apart into sharp splinters, and send your entire family to the hospital or morgue."

It just wasn't fair.

Dark smoke that smelled of rotten eggs billowed out from the SUV's undercarriage. It blanketed the band's plaid red-and-white trailer, clouding its normally bright visage and covering it with a layer of grime.

Ominously symbolic.

With a heavy heart, Slavko took charge. "Junior, get behind the trailer and keep an eye out for someone that might barrel into us. Scream bloody murder if anything's coming."

Wincing at the stench, he pointed to Happy Eddie and Silent Wally. "You two, any ideas what we're looking at?"

When he was a little kid, Slavko had watched his pa work on the family station wagon, the farm's tractor, and other machinery, but had never gotten the mechanical bug. If his tuba worked, that was all he cared. Nonetheless, he joined the other two in bending down and peering at the undercarriage, albeit while covering his nose and mouth with the crook of his sleeve. He didn't know a gasket from a carburetor though he was pretty sure those were part of the engine up front, but he searched for clues anyway. He had to do something.

Happy Eddie slung his bulk partway beneath the undercarriage even as the smoke and its disgusting odor dissipated. He muttered soft curses, coughed, and shook his head. Finally, he pulled himself back out and got to his feet.

"You know me with these things," he said grimly. "I know just enough to be dangerous. So take all this with a grain of salt. Keeping that in mind, back here we could be talking anything from control arm bushings to ball joints to struts. By the way it sounded—all that clanging and grinding— I'd guess a busted axle. But that smell of sulfur could be the axle seals leaking and getting on the brakes. Maybe it's one or the other. Maybe both. Or something else entirely."

Maybe both.

Slavko felt his head explode. Green dollar signs erupted before his mind's eye, billowing up into a mushroom-shaped cloud, then detonated and rained down like blood-red confetti.

Just take me out and shoot me. Stick a fork in us. We're done.

He closed his eyes, rubbed his temples, and tried to think. No miracles came to mind. He pulled out his phone and searched for the nearest garage.

Eleven miles away.

"Do you think we can limp to a gas station eleven miles away?" he asked Happy Eddie, knowing the answer but also cringing at the cost of towing the SUV and trailer that far.

"No chance," Happy Eddie said. "I don't think it could make even a mile. We can try if you want to. You're the boss. It's your call. But I doubt very much we'd make it and we could make the damage a lot worse. If it's a busted axle, maybe even total it."

Silent Wally nodded mournfully in apparent agreement, as if at a funeral. The band's funeral.

You're the boss. It's your call. With the shit hitting the fan, no one was looking to make the tough calls now. No more second-guessing, at least until things went wrong. The boys were standing behind him one hundred percent. Letting him be first in the line of fire.

Silent Wally's mournful funereal look spoke volumes as loud as any words.

Had the Pied Piper Polish Polka Dots just been reduced to nothing more than four dead men walking?

———

Two days and more than two thousand dollars later, they were back on the Mass Pike en route to Schenectady, New York.

Crushing. There was no other way to describe it.

The money simply had not been there to cover the costs. All of the charges had been outrageous and disheartening, from the towing to the repairs to the two unexpected nights in a local hotel waiting for the ordered parts to materialize and the work to be completed. Of course, the corresponding two nights of their Schenectady hotel reservation had been nonrefundable so as to get a bargain deal.

The money just kept hemorrhaging.

Slavko had been forced to take one last advance on his own credit card—Mastercard and Visa were not exactly generous when granting credit limits to freelance musicians, much less freelance *polka* musicians—putting himself in serious financial jeopardy, possibly even bankruptcy if the Polka Dots folded. It violated every last piece of business common sense in the book. When an artist went bankrupt, he lost his intellectual property, his work, his art. That could not be an option. At the same time, Slavko believed in the band, whether that made sense or not. And the garage wasn't going to fix the Explorer on Slavko's good looks. It was cash money, Visa, or Mastercard.

So he pulled out his personal Visa card, holding his breath that he hadn't miscalculated that he'd squeak under the limit, and when the charge went through, applied his signature this one last time.

There probably was a song in this. Slavko, though, would never write it. He felt too crushed to even consider putting his thoughts on paper for a future time. It would, of course, be no bouncing, joyful polka. No one would dance to the "No Money, No Friends, No Hope Polka." More likely it would be one of Happy Eddie's country tunes. "Lost it All in Schenectady" as a working title might be a start, Slavko thought grimly.

The only thing that could have been worse was if the repairs had taken yet another day. Then they'd have missed their first of two nights in Schenectady, three shows each night at the Kielbasa Korner. It was a gig that promised a much-needed infusion of cash and high spirits. Nothing could overstate the desperate need for cash on the barrelhead, but coming off all the cancellations and ridicule, the band was also teetering on the verge of emotional bankruptcy. They all were starving for a great show.

They should get that tonight threefold, barring further disaster. But knock on wood, there were no more ominous knocks erupting from the undercarriage. The Explorer was riding smoothly and quietly. They'd arrive at the Kielbasa Korner with more than enough time to set up for the first show.

Knock on wood, knock on wood, knock on wood.

Slavko leaned back into the SUV's seat and took what felt like his millionth recent deep breath. He sipped his lukewarm coffee, put it back in the cupholder, and tried to focus on Blake Shelton singing his latest country hit instead of waiting, muscles tensed, for the sounds of new breakage in the undercarriage.

"Hey, I saw something in the newspaper back before we left Boston," Happy Eddie said. "Couple days old then, about a week old now. The paper was laying there in the hotel lobby next to the coffee. *The Boston Globe.* Meant to give it to you but things got all pissy between us and it didn't seem like the right time. Then this damned clunker broke down and it was up on the lift at the garage. Not that everyone's in a great mood now, but if I keep waiting for that, the paper'll be old and yellow." Without his eyes turning from the road, he fished out a curled-up newspaper from the pocket of the driver's side door.

"Arts section had this profile about a classical violinist promoting her concert," he continued. "You know, one of them hoity-toity types at Symphony Hall. High society. Men wearing suits and ties or even tuxes. Women in evening gowns. Sipping their champagne or chardonnay or cabernet at intermission. Discussing the stock market. Tax shelters. Debentures, whatever the hell they are. Not our crowd, I know. Nobody wearing checkered flannel shirts and jeans there, drinking lukewarm Budweiser.

"But it still got me thinking we could try doing more of that publicity ourselves. I know you send out press releases and we're on the opposite side of the snooty fence from those classical folks. And God knows none of us is as pretty as that cute thing, the violinist, which is kind of how it caught my eye, to tell you the truth. Saw her picture and had to read what she was about. But it's an idea."

Slavko nodded, doubting there was much more he could do in promotion than what he'd been trying for years. Polka was simply the toughest of sells except in tiny geographic niches with the right ethnic makeup. The Grammy Awards were right to dump them. But the way things were going, he couldn't shut down any ideas. So he readied himself to go through the motions.

Slavko unfurled the curled-up newspaper and held up the wrinkled pages to pretend to read every last word. Blah, blah, blah, blah. Blah, blah, blah, blah.

His gaze fell upon the violinist's photograph. It was hard to miss, filling the upper right half of the page, just below the headline "La Petite Rockette Set To Take Off."

His jaw dropped. He stared at the photograph, unable to tear his eyes away.

Slavko could not believe what he saw.

Slavko stared at the black-and-white photograph in *The Boston Globe*. It filled the upper right half of the wrinkled page, just below the headline "La Petite Rockette Set To Take Off."

Slavko couldn't believe his eyes. The resemblance was stunning. Impossible.

His goddess had made no secret that she wore a disguise. She'd flaunted it. Especially the conspicuously fake, rust-colored wig. But also the bright red lipstick, the garish purple eye shadow, and the exaggerated makeup on her high cheekbones. Not to mention the librarian's fake black-rimmed eyeglasses that inevitably fell off or were discarded as soon as their lovemaking got hot and heavy.

Slavko mentally removed all the fakery—the eyeglasses, the extreme makeup, and the almost comical wig—and replaced it with the image in the black-and-white photograph: bright eyes, normal skin tones, and long, jet-black hair tied back.

A shocking resemblance.

Could it be?

With mounting excitement, he flattened the wrinkled paper against his thigh. Looked closer.

Could it be? His heart pounded in his chest. *It was!*

This was more than a resemblance. This *was* his goddess! His head swam at the realization.

His goddess was—he checked the photo's caption—her name was Julia Chu! She had a name! And a life outside of the bedroom they'd shared! A life with a history and wants and desires and dreams.

An extraordinary life, it seemed. Without even reading a word of the article, Slavko could tell. Extraordinary. *A musician!* And not just any musician. World class! She was...

His goddess was—

"She's a looker, ain't she?" Happy Eddie said with a coarse laugh, yanking Slavko back to his shotgun seat in the Explorer, shattering his joyful mood. Back to the smell of coffee and egg sandwiches and even worse, someone passing gas in the back seat. Back to the seat belt tight across his chest. Back to the remnant bitter traces of the cheap coffee in his mouth.

Slavko blinked.

The unwelcome interruption annoyed him—why couldn't Happy Eddie shut the hell up?—but even so, Slavko rejoiced.

He knew who his goddess was! Julia Chu! *La Petite Rockette!*

And with that, there was a chance!

Slavko looked at Happy Eddie, then back at the photo.

"You look like a teenage boy who just opened his first *Playboy*,"

Happy Eddie said, a smirk visible through his Santa Claus beard. "Good to see you finally with a smile on your face."

The comment annoyed Slavko. Not because Happy Eddie was laughing at him—that was fine—but because it didn't seem properly respectful of his goddess. *La Petite Rockette!* He supposed that emotion was silly since the way he'd met her—had met...*Julia!*—had been far more risqué than a *Playboy* centerfold. Even so, Slavko felt an odd, instinctive need to defend her honor.

He frowned, fumbled for the right words, and came up empty. Finally, he muttered, "Keep your eyes on the damned road!"

Happy Eddie responded with a snort. The boys in back snickered.

It had been a weak retort. Slavko knew it and so did the boys. He slouched down in his seat and narrowed his eyes. Trying not to appear overly interested, Slavko began to read the article.

The more he read, the harder it was to feign disinterest. His goddess, Julia, was apparently one of the top solo violinists in the world. He supposed as a musician he should know that, but the worlds of classical and polka music simply did not meet.

There was no intersection. Only parallel highways. Although Slavko had to admit, Julia's was a six-lane, freshly paved, superhighway, and his was...a dirt road filled with potholes, rocks, and weeds, the jalopy ahead kicking up clouds of smoke.

He shook his head in frustration. Enough of that talk. There was nothing to be gained by it.

The important thing, the vital thing, was that he knew who his goddess was! It even began to dawn on him why she'd been so adamant that she maintain her privacy. Hold tight her secrets. Let no one know, least of all him, her true identity.

Slavko supposed that in the hoity-toity world of classical music with its suits and ties and evening gowns and champagne, satisfying one's wanton desires was best kept behind closed doors, if satisfied at all. Especially for a woman. The double standard surely existed in the old-fashioned polka world, but his impression of the patrons of Bach, Beethoven, and Mozart was that they assumed their shit didn't stink and presumed their virginal female musicians did nothing more randy than slink off to bed alone after their final encores.

Well, Julia's secrets were safe with him. He would never betray her trust.

He just had to first earn that trust. And to do that, they had to somehow meet again.

Shoving the curled-up newspaper into the side pocket of his door with feigned nonchalance—though God help anyone who tried to take it from him—Slavko pulled his phone out of his jeans pocket. He angled his body slightly and held the phone sideways to shield it from potentially peering eyes.

As he pulled up the Google app, his breathing quickened. His mouth suddenly felt dry as cotton. Slavko licked his lips.

Into the search window, he typed, "Julia Chu tour schedule."

Chapter Eleven

Despite the floor-to-ceiling glass wall providing a perfect view of the Philadelphia skyline, Julia felt the walls of her luxurious hotel suite closing in on her. She needed to escape its jaws. Get outside and breathe fresh air. The darkness she'd felt since arriving in the city on Monday had grown the next day, and now on Wednesday, the day before the introductory rehearsal with the orchestra, it was reaching a dissonant crescendo.

After an absurdly priced room service breakfast of scrambled eggs and toast that she'd barely picked at, choosing instead to mostly just sip her artificially sweetened coffee, Julia had hung the Do Not Disturb sign on her room door and practiced for three hours.

A perfect three hours?

Close. But close wasn't good enough. Not when perfection was expected. Or in truth, not just expected.

Demanded.

If not from the critics, many of whom salivated like rabid dogs at the very thought of writing scathing reviews that toppled iconic artists from their lofty pedestals, and if not from the endless supply of jealous competitors nipping at her heels, then from herself. Her own worst critic. The one she could never truly satisfy.

She'd been technically flawless throughout the three hours. No one could critique her technique. But it had been soullessly perfect technique. The fire and passion that made her *La Petite Rockette* had been missing. Even when she'd tried to summon it.

In theory, passion-free technical perfection was acceptable during practice. Actually desirable. To fill every note in every hour of practice with performance-level passion was too exhausting. Far too much intensity. An artist would burn out. Burn to a crisp. So during her practice hours, Julia picked her spots according to a carefully scripted plan, summoning the passion when the time was right. The ideal balance.

Today, however, she'd been barely able to summon it at all and when she had, she'd lost it fast. Which terrified her. You performed how you practiced. If she allowed this dark malaise to invade her practice hours on a regular basis, preventing her from summoning the passion on demand, then sooner or later it would infect her performance on the concert stage.

No more *La Petite Rockette.*

With the suite's walls closing in on her, Julia robotically wiped down the Stradivarius, a smooth cloth on the wooden frame and another to clean the rosin off the strings. Cradling the priceless instrument gently like a mother would her infant, she rested it in its padded case, locked the case, and then placed the case in the suite's oversized safe at the far right edge of the closet.

If only she could talk to the Stradivarius and get its sage advice. In a book or a movie, she supposed she would have named the priceless instrument. Probably a masculine name, something exotic like Jacques, Cristiano, or Bertrand. Or if she had a truly warped sense of humor, Brad.

Brad the Strad.

Yeah, that would work. Julia gave that thought a brief snicker. Or would it be a feminine name? Monique, Raquel, or Simone.

Of course, only a madwoman would even think about talking to her violin. And Julia was no madwoman.

But who else could she talk to?

She picked up her phone off the nightstand charger, and since she always silenced it while practicing, unmuted it.

No messages.

She flopped down onto the bed, her head on the stack of three soft pillows and her legs hanging off the side, and pressed the phone icon. She scanned her list of favorites, but there was no one with whom she could unburden her dark soul.

And isn't that a sad commentary!

Her two closest friends at the conservatory, Yiwei Zhang and Amada Fachiri, had remained musical soulmates with whom she could confide all her deepest fears and darkest moments. That is, until Julia's career ascended and theirs did not. What had been mutual support for each other—shoulders to cry on and thoughtful advice or perspective when one of them couldn't see the forest for the trees—had become subtle sabotage as jealousy turned both relationships toxic. Passive aggressive comments designed to undercut Julia's confidence. Whispered lies to others about her. A submerged but still detectable joy at her failures. Finally, Julia had been forced to cut them off. Blocked their emails and phone numbers. Out of her life entirely.

She needed a friend like Yiwei and Amanda had once been, a musical soulmate, but none remained anymore. And as an only child, there wasn't a loving sister to contact either.

Julia's finger instinctively hovered over the entry for her mother. It was an odd choice. They'd already completed their regularly scheduled weekly chat a couple days ago. It would be strange and out of character to call again so soon. Julia dutifully honored both her parents, paying special tribute to them in every media interview, but there wasn't the kind of intimate relationship Julia heard of other daughters having with their mother. Her mother was more of a stern taskmaster and Julia, her submissive, gifted, but sadly imperfect student, never deserving of more than an A-minus grade.

The darkness Julia felt was not something she could discuss with her. Never in a million years. With anyone but Mother.

But with no better alternative, Julia pressed the icon. She had no idea what she would say—"I was just thinking about talking to my violin" was most definitely *not* a possibility—and Julia considered hanging up after the first ring.

Instead, the phone rang until it went to voicemail.

"It's just me, Julia," she said, and then hung up, knowing there'd been no need to identify herself. Her mother's phone would take care of that. In fact, it had been silly to even leave a message. Her mother called whenever she spotted a missed call.

"That was a mistake," Julia muttered, feeling relief at the missed connection, not disappointment, but knowing she'd have to be ready to explain why she'd called when her mother got back to her.

Julia clicked to see her list of recent calls. Almost all of them were from her booking manager, Lisa McCarthy, a perky, twenty-five-year-old, brunette fireball who did whatever she was told but sometimes never shut up.

This was most definitely not a discussion for her either. Julia kept Lisa at arm's length, paying her a handsome flat fee to handle all the booking and publicity details, but Lisa was no friend. Julia had learned that lesson the hard way years ago when she considered her manager—Emily Franklin, who'd fancied herself an agent, not just a mere manager—to be her closest friend and confidante only to discover after several years that Emily had embezzled more than half of Julia's money. The financial equivalent of Xiangyu Lee. And in truth, emotionally almost as devastating.

Never again.

After that and her disheartening experiences with her former classmates at the conservatory, Julia had decided that no one would get close to her. She would be an island. No one would get access to her checking account. And no one would get access to her heart.

Which left her at times like these painfully alone. A barren island made of nothing but dry, windswept sand.

"I don't even have an agent to steal from me," Julia muttered with a bittersweet laugh, then shook her head.

I really have no one, she thought. *Push everyone away and this is what you get.*

The sadness inside her soul deepened. Was this what she really wanted?

The answer burst through the surface of her conscious.

Slavko.

She'd tried to ignore it, but his name had been percolating below the surface for hours. No, not hours. Days. Ever since she'd sent him out that hotel room door.

Julia closed her eyes and could see him in her mind's eye. The shy smile and soft green eyes. The broad shoulders and barrel chest. His thick, dark, wavy hair. The taste of mint on his magical lips when he kissed her. The smell of his cologne, cedarwood with hints of nutmeg and citrus.

Slavko.

She could feel his presence. He was more than just the mere boy toy who had satisfied her every sexual desire. He had won her heart.

Julia wished he was here right now, lying beside her, holding her in his tight embrace. Kissing her. Caressing her. Loving her.

Stop it!

She leapt off the bed. Hadn't she already convinced herself that Slavko was the Serpent in her Garden of Eden? She walked over to the wide oak desk and stared at the words she written on the memo pad in the upper left corner.

Slavko is the Serpent!

He would ruin her. Even more completely than Xiangyu Lee had. In fact, wasn't there a near certainty that the dark malaise she felt today—and the day before that, and the day before that day—was entwined with her longing for Slavko?

Entwined as tightly as they'd been physically entwined. Entwined as tightly as her heart now felt toward him.

Stop it!

Slavko is the Serpent! Slavko is the Serpent! Slavko is the Serpent!

Julia rushed to the expansive closet that ran half the length of the wall, looked past all her carefully hung dress clothes, and yanked out of her suitcase a pair of baggy gray sweatpants and an equally drab hoodie, running shoes, a winter wool cap to tuck her hair inside, and the fake librarian glasses she'd worn when she met...when she met...

Slavko.

No!

Slavko, the Serpent! The Serpent! The Serpent! The Serpent!

In her drab disguise, Julia walked aimlessly through the mall. In Saks Off 5th, she tried on a glittery black blouse with matching slacks that fit her like a glove. The combination looked perfect, a sure-fire purchase on any other day, but today she glumly put them both on their racks.

Didn't feel like it.

She sniffed designer perfumes with exotic French names and descriptions. *Dolce & Gabbana's Velvet Pure Eau de Parfum. Amouage's Ashore Eau De Parfum.* And *Lalique's Les Compositions Parfumees Leather Copper Eau De Parfum.* They flooded her senses with a fleeting pleasure, but she bought none.

After several other high-end clothing stores, Julia meandered into an Olympia Sports store. Probably, she figured, because she'd scheduled an hour this afternoon in the hotel gym—officially called a salon, but she wasn't going for a massage or pedicure—and her subconscious was scolding her for planning to skip it.

Yes, she told herself, she really needed the exercise. Was overdue, in fact. Skip it too many times and her enemies would no doubt suggest a replacement for the *La Petite Rockette* nickname. Something like *L'enorme Rockette.* Then their snide suggestions that her looks were the major reason for her success would be put to the test.

No exercise, no more *"Petite."* No passion, no more *"Rockette."*

The end of *La Petite Rockette.*

Julia wanted to scream. She raced out of the store and noticed a sign for a cinema at the end of the mall.

Escape. Just what she needed. She'd say to hell with her overly scripted schedule and fall head over heels into the kind of escape Hollywood specialized in.

Julia bought a ticket for the next movie showing of the fourteen offered, a Sandra Bullock feature, one hopefully full of laughs. Julia felt she could use a few laughs right now. She stopped at the concession stand and bought a large popcorn with extra butter.

To hell with *petite*. To hell with *La Petite Rockette*. To hell with it all.

Julia took her seat and shoveled the buttery, salty popcorn into her mouth. Then shoveled in some more.

Twenty minutes into the movie, tears pooled in her eyes. The emptiness she felt inside was about to explode.

Bad choice of movie. Not just a comedy. A romantic comedy with Bullock as a one-dimensional woman obsessed with her career with no time for love.

Not just too close to home. It felt to Julia like a bull's-eye with love's arrow shot through her heart. She raced out of the theater, choking back tears. She was such a cliché that Hollywood wrote about pathetic women like her.

In the movie, there would be a happy ending for her cliché of a character. There was always a happy ending.

But not for her. For her, no happy ending was possible. She'd been faced with her choice. Her music or love. And she'd made her choice, dammit. She'd made her choice.

No happily ever after.

Julia raced through the mall, not sure where she was going, not paying attention to the stores she passed, not caring about the smells of the foods or the buzz of voices.

It was all a blur.

Julia noticed nothing until for some reason, surely masochistic, she spotted out of the corner of her eye a couple huddled at a table inside a café just thirty feet away. At first glance, the man looked much like Slavko. Broad-shouldered with thick, dark, wavy hair parted on the side. And a wonderful warm smile he was showering on the woman, who looked nothing like Julia at all. Caucasian. Voluptuous. Long, ash-blond hair. Smiling. Happy.

Not like Julia at all.

The man who looked like Slavko, but wasn't, leaned forward across the table, smiling, taking the woman's hand. The happy woman, so unlike Julia, followed suit, and they kissed.

Short and sweet.

Wonderful.

Almost in unison, they frowned and turned to look at Julia. She was frozen in place, staring at them.

Julia broke free of her trance and raced away, thinking that she'd been wrong. Her life was no Garden of Eden.

She wanted the Serpent.

Chapter Twelve

A huge grin spread across Slavko's face. No matter how hard he tried to hide it, it grew wider and wider. His heart felt ready to burst. He wanted to shout in euphoric jubilation. And if he weren't sitting in the Explorer, its tires humming along the Mass Pike and its stuffy confines filled with warm, stale air and the sounds of country music, he'd thrust his clenched fists to the sky in victory and leap for joy.

Jackpot!

He'd doubted he would ever see his goddess—*Julia!*—again. Aside from the not-so-minor problem that she'd indicated they were through—yeah, just a wee bit of an issue there—he'd figured there was no way he could reconcile his hopes with the band's meandering path through states from Pennsylvania and New York to Ohio, Michigan, and Wisconsin, then down to Texas and off to Colorado. Their tour had them playing more than two hundred dates over the next year and nowhere close to Boston, where he'd originally assumed Julia lived. What were the odds that tour would intersect with wherever Julia might be?

Until Happy Eddie's crumpled copy of the *Boston Globe* pointed him to her identity, Slavko was at the mercy of the anonymous hook-up app just to communicate with her. And even if she did check the app, saw his message and chose, wonder of wonders, not to follow through with her painfully stated intentions to avoid him, they would almost certainly be hundreds and hundreds of miles apart with no chance of another meeting.

And that was if she was even willing to see him again. Which she'd made clear was...not...going...to...happen. Despite what had felt like a magnetic attraction for each other. One that transcended even the mind-boggling sex they had enthusiastically enjoyed.

He'd had no chance at all.

Until now.

The odds were still stacked against him—she had, after all, said that they were through and if that was truly what she wanted, he'd have to honor that—but for the first time since she'd all but pushed him out that hotel room door, they had a chance.

Slim. Maybe even microscopic. But a chance.

In just two weeks, Julia would be appearing in Buffalo, New York. Three shows on Friday through Sunday with the Buffalo Philharmonic Orchestra. The same week that the Pied Piper Polish Polka Dots would be putting the final touches on an extended Oktoberfest at the Buffalo Beer Junction on Thursday and Friday, followed by the Wings & Kielbasa Bar on Saturday and Sunday.

He and Julia, both in Buffalo on the same weekend! Close enough to kiss. Almost.

Fate was shining on them! They were meant for each other! He knew it!

He would—

"Spit it out, man! What's the good news?"

Slavko jumped with a start, yanked from his thoughts. He blinked rapidly, unsure where the unwelcome noise had come from.

His mind came back to his surroundings: the Explorer in the leftmost of the three lanes of the Mass Pike, passing a FedEx eighteen-wheeler, the country song "Beer Never Broke my Heart" playing on the radio.

Happy Eddie, whose voice had pulled Slavko from his reveries, muted the radio. Happy Eddie beamed. "If that isn't news about a great new gig then I'll be dipped in shit and roasted on a stick! I can tell from the look on your face. Tell us, man! What's the good news?"

Slavko felt the huge smile drop off his face. His euphoria remained over the mere possibility of seeing Julia again. Nothing could extinguish that. That brightened even his darkest thoughts. Happy Eddie, however, had sapped away a measure of that giddy delight by yanking Slavko back to reality, reminding him of the band's dire circumstances and by extension, his own impending financial ruin.

Slavko blinked. He didn't know what to say. There was no good news to share.

Happy Eddie frowned.

"I've known you since you were knee-high to a grasshopper," Happy Eddie said without taking his eyes from the road. "And you don't go from looking like your dog died to acting like you just hit the lottery without getting the most gigantic good news we've seen in a long, long time. We could sure use a lift, man. Don't hold out on us."

"It's...um...personal," Slavko said, forcing a weak grin. "Nothing about the band."

Happy Eddie's face fell. His shoulders slumped.

"Damn. Damn, damn, damn," Happy Eddie said. "Hey, I'm happy for you and all that, whatever the news is, but the way you lit up there gave me hope we just might make it after all, at least to the end of this tour."

"Sorry," Slavko said. He'd felt such euphoria that he might actually see Julia again. It had flooded all his inner being with a warmth that he'd been no more able to conceal than a five-year-old's excitement on Christmas morning. He felt badly that he'd inadvertently toyed with Happy Eddie's emotions, so he added words he wasn't quite sure he believed. "We're going to make it. And not just to the end of the tour."

Happy Eddie shot him a look of, if not outright disbelief, then at least substantial doubt. But he said nothing.

Silence fell heavy once again inside the claustrophobic vehicle, the warm air feeling as lifeless as the other band members' emotions.

"Let me guess," Happy Eddie finally said after a time. "Your Boston chick ain't lost and gone forever after all, dear Clementine. She's back. And she meeting you in Schenectady tonight and you're gonna play Romeo and commandeer the vehicle again."

Slavko recoiled. Was he that transparent?

"Don't call her 'that Boston chick!'" he snapped. "Show some respect! Her name is—"

Slavko's eyes widened. *Whoa, that had been close.*

Happy Eddie stole a quick expectant glance, then looked back at the road. Slavko sensed the boys in the back hunching forward.

The silence in the Explorer seemed to pulse with either anticipation or tension, Slavko wasn't sure which.

"Her name," Slavko finally said, "is none of your damned business. And no, I'm not meeting her tonight in Schenectady, and I'm not commandeering the Explorer."

Which was true, he supposed, but a major-league lie of omission and one that could come back to bite him. If he actually pulled off a miracle, he'd be meeting Julia not tonight in Schenectady nor a few nights later in nearby Albany, but the following week in Buffalo. And depending on the circumstances, he might need to commandeer the Explorer. Happy Eddie had come uncomfortably close to a bull's-eye.

Slavko wondered if he should amend his blanket denial. Give himself some wiggle room in case he did pull off the miracle. But what should he say?

"Fair enough, I stand corrected," Happy Eddie said, his playful grin gone, replaced by a somber look. "But I gotta say I am concerned. It feels like the band is going down the drain, then I see you looking all excited so I think we've finally gotten some good news. But turns out, it's *personal.* No good news for the band. You're just all dreamy-eyed like a high school girl with a crush. Your head in the clouds, a million miles from the problems we're dealing with. A lovestruck smile on your lips like you're about to embrace the love of your life. It gets me wondering—"

"Sorry!" Slavko snapped, feeling defensive, angry, and snarky all at the same time. Anger and snark won out. "I'll keep any happiness I ever feel in the future to myself!"

He felt guilty as soon as the words were out of his mouth, then felt worse when he saw Happy Eddie wince. But before Slavko could amend his words, Happy Eddie jumped in.

"Hey, be happy. Knock yourself out," he said in an even tone belied by his knuckles turning white in a panicked grip on the steering wheel. "Have your fun times. Get your rocks off. Find true love, if such a thing really exists. We'll all be happy for you, me more than anyone. You know that."

Slavko went to respond but Happy Eddie was on a roll, and like the eighteen-wheelers barreling down this highway, was not to be cut off.

"Just don't be thinking with your dick," Happy Eddie said. "This band is teetering on the edge of a cliff. We're on the precipice. You know it. I know it. And the boys in the back know it." His voice grew thick with emotion. "This life on the road is all I've ever known. It's all I want. I'm nothing without it. Music is all I got. I'm depending on you. We all are."

Slavko felt a fresh set of emotions wash over him. Love for and devotion to all the boys and especially Happy Eddie. They were all in this boat together.

"I won't let you down," Slavko said.

When they took a bathroom break at the next rest stop on the Pike, Slavko gave each of the boys an uncharacteristic hug as they got out of the vehicle. Damn, he loved this band. Loved these guys. He ordered a large cheese pizza for them all to share on his dime. There would only be two slices for each of them—barely an appetizer for Happy Eddie and still a bit short of a bellyful for the rest of them during flush times—but it would be better than nothing.

Slavko wanted to offer the pizza as a peace offering of sorts. Not that he'd done anything explicitly wrong beyond snapping at them a few times, but he wasn't telling them—not yet, at least—about Julia and Buffalo and that he might well be commandeering the Explorer despite the implied denial in his lie of omission. He felt guilty about that deception, but right now he felt like a juggler who was balancing as many flaming torches as he could manage. No need to take on yet another torch unless he pulled off the miracle that would turn his potential gray area of dishonesty into a reality he had to confess.

And frankly, if he could pull off the miracle, the boys could each take an extra flaming torch or ten and *throw* them at him for all he cared. Because that would mean he'd be seeing Julia again.

He'd told the boys he was ordering the pizza, but they still cheered when he brought it to them as they stood outside the Explorer getting a few last gulps of chilly but fresh air. They climbed inside and soon the air smelled deliciously of cheese, tomato, and garlic. Slavko was salivating as much as the others and could have easily wolfed down most of the pizza himself, but after devouring his first slice, he pointed to his other allotted piece and nodded to Happy Eddie.

"Take it, Big Man," Slavko said. "Gotta fatten you up for Christmas."

Happy Eddie grinned broadly, looking like the happiest of Santas. "I'd kiss you, Slavko, if you weren't so ugly."

Slavko blew a mocking kiss, and after Happy Eddie scarfed down the extra slice, he slid the vehicle into drive, and they were off.

Slavko waited as long as he could, staring nonchalantly out the window as they rushed past thick woods of pine, maple, and birch. He managed to wait ten minutes before casually pulling out his phone, lasting that long only by mentally composing his message to Julia.

Painful honesty on his part would be to confess that he had uncovered her identity, one she'd tried so hard to conceal. And that with her identity exposed, he saw that her concert schedule placed her in Buffalo the same weekend that he'd be there. He was dying to be with her again. Could she please give him one more chance? He wouldn't be pushy and use the clearly forbidden "love" word.

Painful honesty would even force him to confess that he was so smitten with her that he intended to read every last story on the Internet about her. Devouring the stories like Happy Eddie and his extra slice of pizza. Slavko would read every last word before Buffalo because he wanted to know everything about her. And of course, he'd believe only the good stuff, none of the bad.

All of that would be painfully honest. Truthful to a fault. But it wouldn't just be painfully honest. It would be suicidal.

He had scared her away with his mere request for her name or anything at all about herself. Then told her his own name and that he'd freely tell her his entire life story, which had totally freaked her out. And then sealed his doom—at least for that night, Slavko hoped to God it wasn't for forever—when he'd told her he couldn't get enough of her.

Told her he *loved* her.

Painful honesty.

Suicidal honesty.

He wouldn't make that mistake again if he got a second chance. Because he knew for certain, if he blew it this time, there would be no third opportunity.

Slavko silenced his phone so there would be no audible clicks as he typed. As casually as possible, he angled his body and the phone away from the six potentially prying eyes in the Explorer. Even so, he felt those eyes peering over his shoulder. If they read his words, eyes would widen. Jaws drop. Anger explode. All because of his lies of omission.

I'm not meeting her tonight in Schenectady, and I'm not comman-deering the Explorer.

But no one was peering over his shoulder. The eyes he felt and the reactions he imagined were in his mind alone. Junior, directly behind Slavko, was playing a video game. Silent Wally, diagonally behind Slavko, wasn't completely silent. He was softly snoring. Happy Eddie was focused on the road ahead. Only Slavko could see his own words.

He hated them all.

Lies of omission to his brothers. Even worse, lies of omission to Julia. Unavoidable, but still lies.

No rationalization could fix it.

Many men, he knew, used the phrase "what she doesn't know won't hurt her" as an excuse to deceive and dishonor women. Slavko loathed those men and the phrase. But in this case, Julia had left him with no choice. In his message, he had to put into practice that loathsome phrase —he had to deceive her and keep her in the dark—or scare her away.

Did the end justify the means? Slavko wondered if he was just another scumbag taking the easy way out, telling himself that his white lies were well intentioned.

But did he have a choice?

Slavko didn't think so.

He could only make the unspoken promise to Julia, and to himself, that he would never dishonor her and that those lies of omission would never be used as a matter of convenience or to conceal outright dishonesty. His white lies would only be a means to get them together.

And if he managed to get them together, he would make Julia the happiest woman on Earth.

His unsteady finger hovered over the Send button for what felt like eternity. Beads of sweat formed on his forehead. *Please let this work. Just give me a chance. Just one more chance.*

Slavko pressed send.

Chapter Thirteen

ears pooled in Julia's eyes, blurring her vision. People jostled against her as she stood frozen at the Walmart entrance in her drab gray hoodie and sweatpants, hair tucked up into her equally drab gray woolen cap, her fake librarian glasses sliding down her nose. The smells of stale sweat and perfume filled the air.

"Get out of the way!" scolded a stick-thin teenaged girl with acne on her forehead, as she elbowed past Julia. "Goddamned Chinese! Think they own the country!"

Robotically, Julia moved away from the store entrance, not sure why she had stopped there in the first place, not remembering why she'd come to the mall at all, only vaguely registering the racism sent her way. She leaned heavily against the store's rough brick wall.

Slavko. Julia could think of nothing else. *Slavko.*

She wanted him. She needed him. Even if he was the Serpent.

She didn't need to be like the Sandra Bullock character in the movie, a one-dimensional woman obsessed with her career with no time for love. A Hollywood cliché. She could choose a different path.

She held out her phone, knowing she had to press the icon for DiscreetPartnerForYou and try to contact him before she changed her mind. But the tears pooling in her eyes blurred her vision and her hand shook so badly, she couldn't make out even the most familiar icons on her phone. And she certainly couldn't risk being overheard using voice activation for a scandalous app like that.

Julia raced back to her hotel, everything a blur, trying to shield her face from any clusters of people with a hand to her temple, hoping no one would take a photograph of her looking like this. She navigated the hotel lobby and breathed a sigh of relief when she stepped into the elevator alone. She stabbed the button for her floor over and over to no effect until she remembered she needed to use the electronic card for her room to gain access to her floor. Choking back a sob, she fumbled for it in her sweatpants pocket, swiped it, got to her floor, then ran down the carpeted hallway to her room.

Julia stumbled into her darkened room, tears streaming down her face, letting loose the sobs. She gave them free rein, slumping to the floor in the darkness. Her back was up against the wall, elbows on her knees so she could hold her head in her hands.

She had felt the need to escape this elegant suite, but her dark mood of abject loneliness had followed her. Into shops at the mall that held clothes and jewelry and perfumes that she should want but had lost her desire for. Into the Sandra Bullock movie that had sent Julia fleeing for the exit because she knew a happy ending awaited Bullock as the romantic comedy's heroine but none awaited her. And past that couple in the café —the man who at first glance had looked so much like Slavko it had pierced her heart, but the woman so unlike herself—the couple that had it all.

That couple was enjoying their own Garden of Eden. Or maybe it was a tough life filled with problems, but they at least had each other. And they knew that meant everything. She could see it in their smiling faces, the love in their eyes, and the kiss they shared.

Julia wanted that.

In the darkness of this luxury suite she could see with utter clarity that this life of hers was no Garden of Eden. Not anymore. She'd thought she had it all, was living the most perfect life possible, but the Serpent had showed her the emptiness of this life and how utterly alone she was. The

Serpent—Slavko!—had shown himself to be the one thing this supposed Garden of Eden denied her.

And the one thing she needed the most.

Julia needed Slavko.

Sniffing, she swiped away the tears on her wet cheeks with a bare palm and got slowly to her feet. She scanned the illuminated panel next to the door and pressed the round "All Lights On" button. The lights in the room all grew gradually brighter as if an electronic knob was being turned with the exactly appropriate speed. Not too slow. Not too fast. The curtains that covered the floor-to-ceiling glass wall automatically parted, giving way to the perfect view of the Philadelphia skyline that had given her no joy before she left and provided none now that she had returned.

Julia collapsed into the desk chair and pulled up the DiscreetPartner-ForYou app on her phone. As it slowly came up, she thought of what she might say in her message to Slavko. She certainly wouldn't reveal her identity or provide her entire tour schedule so that he might figure out who she was. But perhaps a location or two on the tour. Better yet, she could query him for his location and she would fly there early in the week in time to return for the rehearsals and weekend concerts.

But when the app came up, the envelope widget showed red with the number two superimposed on it. There were two messages. They had to be from Slavko. Her settings on the app mandated automatically deleting messages from anyone but her specified list. A list that was usually empty, but she'd set to include Slavko for their times together in Boston and had not returned to the app since they parted.

A subconscious omission? She'd removed every previous boy toy— there had been half a dozen—almost as soon as they were out of her hotel room door. She'd wanted no pleas for a second night together or even a request to continue correspondence. One and done. That had been her rule.

Until Slavko.

Julia clicked on the envelope widget and saw there were, in fact, two messages from him, both from earlier today, several hours apart. With shaking hands, Julia clicked to read the first one.

Chapter Fourteen

The silence was deafening.

Not literally. The Kielbasa Korner Bar was exploding in a cacophony of noise as the boys crashed and banged their way through setting up for the seven o'clock show, stomping up the side stairs to the forty-foot-wide stage in the rear while carrying microphones, stands, amplifiers, speakers, and their instruments. A steady hum of conversation in the half-filled bar rose and fell, punctuated by laughter or the slamming down of a beer mug by a patron at one of the dozen tables or sitting on a stool at the bar that extended all the way down the right wall. Behind the bar, a large flat-screen TV blared a major league baseball playoff game while beside it another one silently displayed Keno. On the opposite wall, another muted TV showed ESPN SportsCenter. Two broad-shouldered waitresses in Bavarian barmaid garb took orders and hustled drinks from the bartender and food from the kitchen to the tables.

More than enough noise to choke a mule. Presumably, the baseball game would be muted once the show began, the first of three performances that evening with another three the following night. It would be up to the Pied Piper Polish Polka Dots to draw attention away from the TVs and silence the conversation and laughter with their music. With any luck, they'd get couples dancing joyfully in the meager open floor space

90

between the elevated stage and the tables. Room enough for little more than a dozen of them. Please, God, Slavko thought, let that space be crowded or at least not empty. Please let the band be playing to an appreciative audience and not a bunch of drunks who wanted them silenced and the TV turned up to full volume.

The smell of beer, cheeseburgers, and kielbasa filled the air. A Polish specialty like kielbasa and the handwritten whiteboards on the walls promoting the Kielbasa Special of the Day were promising signs. Although Slavko liked to believe that all audiences could enjoy polka if they just gave it a chance, its appeal inevitably went along ethnic lines, most notably Polish, Czech, Slovenian, German, and Slovakian. He was the only band member who was not Polish, and he was Slovakian. Hopefully, the band's rattled spirits—and their wallets since they'd been promised a share of the take—would be lifted by an enthusiastic reception in a packed house, a raucous time at the bar for all three shows on both nights. Slavko begged the gods of music for it.

But not as hard, nowhere near as hard, as he begged the gods of love —Cupid, Eros, Aphrodite or whoever they were—for an answer from Julia. He'd sent her his first message earlier that day shortly after the cheese pizza rest stop and been greeted with total silence. He knew it was being unrealistic to expect an immediate response, but he couldn't help himself. Every minute of silence felt like years. With a sinking heart, he'd sent another message, promising both her and himself that it would be his last, at least for the next few weeks. He would be no stalker.

Crickets.

If a phone icon could actually be worn out, he'd have crushed the one for DiscreetPartnerForYou, checking it over and over again, so often that it had caught Happy Eddie's unfortunate attention as Slavko walked back to the band's trailer for another load.

"Like a high school girl waiting by the phone," Happy Eddie said with what was surely a teasing grin. "Hoping her true love will call."

Slavko glared. It was undoubtedly the sort of playful ball busting that he would have laughed at in another time and place. But not now. Now, he was in no mood for anything but a response from Julia.

He changed his settings on the DiscreetPartnerForYou app to send him a notification if any message came in. There'd be no need to check the app every five minutes or four or three. Minutes that felt like eons. If Julia responded to him, he'd get the ping of an alert along with a discreet message from the ambiguously identified text message. He always shut off his phone during performances, of course, but he also hated the idea of a ping coming in at some other wrong time, forcing him to give a cover story to the boys. It was why he'd held off on the setting change in the first place, but the suspense—the overwhelming *longing* to get a response from Julia—was killing Slavko. He couldn't stand it any longer.

There was no ping for a text message. Still.

Slavko checked the app again. Nothing there either. He double-checked the new settings. They were correct. He wouldn't have to go to the app to have his heart crushed every five minutes. There was no need. The silence of no text ping was doing that all by itself.

He rebooted the phone, brought in another load from the trailer, and checked again.

Nothing.

It was time to face facts. Julia was simply not going to respond. Whatever he thought he'd read in her face and her actions and her caresses back in Boston had been a mirage. Fool's gold. He'd taken his own emotions and superimposed them on her.

She's just not that into you. If she was, she would have responded.

It had only been a few hours, of course. There was no reason to assume that she'd even seen the messages. But somehow, perhaps because it meant everything to him, he couldn't help despairing that she'd seen the messages, rolled her eyes, and without hesitation pressed delete.

Why should he be surprised? Disappointed. Crushed. Julia had told him they were through. Her words had been abundantly clear. Through was through. Done was done. Kaput was kaput. He had no intention of being a creep who couldn't take no for an answer. Far too many of them became dangerous both to the woman and themselves.

Slavko fully understood that no meant no.

But had that been what Julia really meant? It seemed to him that her panicked shoving him out of that hotel door had been caused by his unfortunate invasion of her privacy, asking for her name or something about herself. Telling her his name. She hadn't been rejecting him, just what he had done.

One minute, he'd been holding her in her arms, feeling the most wonderful glow of post-lovemaking contentment. The purest joy. Life couldn't be any better. There were no higher peaks of emotion and satisfaction to climb.

Then he'd opened his big mouth.

Even now, he shook his head at the monumental, epic stupidity. *You couldn't leave well enough alone. One of the great moments of your life and you had to screw it all up. Royally screw it up.*

He'd tried to pull back the curtain of secrecy between them and all hell had broken loose. From lying blissfully in her arms to getting shoved out the door, barely given enough time to put his clothes back on.

From the penthouse to the outhouse.

What he wouldn't give to go back in time and zipper his damned big mouth shut. They'd had something special. He knew it. And Julia had known it, too.

But if that was the case, why was his damned phone so silent?

As the clock ticked inexorably closer to performance time, Slavko felt like a wishbone being pulled apart until something snapped. Music was his life. This was what he was put on this Earth to do. His love for it was why he'd made so many sacrifices. And the room was filling up. Not totally packed yet, but getting there.

But not a peep from Julia. In another couple minutes, it would be time to turn off his phone, silencing what was already painfully silent.

"Looking good," Junior said, standing next to one of the speakers sitting atop its metal tripod post. He, like the rest of the band members, was dressed in their trademark plaid red-and-white flannel shirts and black jeans, but his scrawny frame made him look like a scarecrow. He crossed his bony fingers for good luck.

"Definitely," Slavko said with a nod, forcing a smile. "Should be a good one."

But Slavko still felt hollow inside. He pulled out his phone and checked if the growing crowd noise might have caused him to miss a ping.

Nothing.

Happy Eddie, opening his battered black accordion case on a table fifteen feet away, looked at Slavko and shook his head compassionately. "You're killing yourself, my man. A watched pot never boils."

Slavko busied himself adjusting the height of a microphone stand for the fifth time. For the third time, he checked the backdrop with *Pied Piper Polish Polka Dots* superimposed in black over the band's plaid red-and-white pattern, making sure the backdrop was snug against the wall behind them. Then he looked for something else to do. He didn't have the time or patience for Happy Eddie right now.

"Juliet ain't calling," Happy Eddie said.

Slavko's eyes widened. A shiver went up and down his spine. "What did you say?"

But Slavko knew exactly what Happy Eddie had just said. *Happy Eddie knew Julia's name!* Probably remembered it from *The Boston Globe* feature story on her. He'd even commented on her photo. So at some point he had put two and two together and figured everything out.

Slavko's heart leapt into his throat. If he'd had any chance at all with Julia, it was gone now. They'd been head over heels for each other—at least he had been and he was sure Julia had felt the same way—until he'd crossed the line into her privacy. He'd been sure he could repair the damage. If she'd just agree to meet with him, he'd convince her their secret would never go beyond their own lips.

Until now. *Happy Eddie knows! Dammit, he knows!*

Heart aching, Slavko strode toward the big man.

Alarmed, Happy Eddie stepped backwards and threw up both hands in defense. "I didn't mean nothing! I was just busting you!"

Slavko got in Happy Eddie's face, so close he could smell the garlic on the big man's breath. He had all he could do to keep from grasping Happy Eddie's XL flannel shirt and shaking him. With great restraint, Slavko held his clenched fists at his side. Through gritted teeth, he demanded, "What did you say?"

"I didn't mean nothing," Happy Eddie repeated, eyes wide. He glanced sideways to the patrons sitting at their tables. "Let's not make a scene, man."

Slavko took a deep breath and shot a look out of the corner of his eyes. A few people were staring. Not shocked. He hadn't done anything, after all.

Yet.

But Happy Eddie was right. Tonight's first crowd was promising. This was absolutely not the time to make a scene.

Slavko channeled his limited acting skills—he knew Hollywood would never come calling for him—and faked a quick laugh. He turned his body to be between Happy Eddie and the audience and snaked his arm around the big man's shoulder. He slapped it with fake good-natured joviality to complete the charade.

"No scene, big man," Slavko said softly but with an edge in his voice. "Just tell me what you said. *Exactly* what you said."

Happy Eddie blinked rapidly, looking as if he might have a tough time remembering his own name. "I was just—"

"*Exactly* what you said," Slavko demanded in barely more than a whisper, tightly squeezing Happy Eddie's shoulder. "Word for word."

Happy Eddie swallowed slowly. "I said, 'Juliet ain't calling.'" He nodded as if reassuring himself that he'd gotten it right. "You know, I've been calling you Romeo. So I was saying your Juliet ain't calling you. I was just busting you. Maybe trying to protect you a little. Save you some grief. But I didn't mean nothing."

Slavko played the scene back in his head, and as he did, his eyes widened once again, but for a different reason. That was *exactly* what Happy Eddie had said.

Juliet. Not Julia. *Juliet.*

Slavko's shoulders slumped as all the air rushed out of his lungs. What a fool he was! He'd almost gone nuclear—or at least as nuclear as he ever went—thinking Happy Eddie had discovered his secret. Julia's secret. *Their* secret.

"Sorry, man," Slavko said. He squeezed the big man's shoulder and patted it, this time with an affection he really meant. "I've been on edge. My bad. Don't know what got into me." He pulled away and looked at Happy Eddie straight on, a hand on each of the big man's shoulders. "Let's have a great show. Or three."

Happy Eddie nodded warily. "You okay?"

Slavko swallowed the lump in his throat and nodded. Happy Eddie had been right. Right about everything. Hell, even his wisecrack about there being a Juliet had been a near miss spookily close to the target. It was time to focus on the band's business. Not that he hadn't tried as hard as he could for the guys. But he'd been smitten ever since that first night with Julia. All he could think about was her.

But if she had cast him aside—and only an idiot would ignore the obvious evidence of her own words that she'd done exactly that—he needed to move on. Keep his eyes on the prize of his music.

Keep the Pied Piper Polish Polka Dots afloat. And that would begin with a knockout performance in just a few minutes, followed by another two later tonight and three tomorrow.

What he was put on this Earth to do.

Time to wake up and smell the coffee. Time to move on.

His phone pinged.

Chapter Fifteen

Julia's heart pounded with anticipation. She was seated at the hotel suite's wide polished oak desk, the floor-to-ceiling glass wall to her left showing off a Philadelphia skyline that might as well be a solid black wall for all she cared. The blank TV screen hanging on the wall to her right and the framed print of van Gogh's *Starry Night* on her left could have been missing and she wouldn't have noticed.

Her focus was locked solely on the DiscreetPartnerForYou app on her phone. Holding her breath, her every muscle taut with tension, Julia clicked on Slavko's first message.

I'm sorry I came on too strong. I promise I will not repeat that mistake if you decide we can meet again. We had three magical nights together. Why not four? All by your rules. I'll keep my big mouth shut except when ordered by you to use it in certain ways. Haha.

I travel a lot and am committed to continue that, contractually and otherwise. So it won't be easy to meet, but I believe it will be worth it. At least for me and I'm hoping for you, too.

You said that you were leaving Boston. Perhaps our schedules and locations can line up. Here is where I'll be for the next month.

A list filling every weekend and many weekdays followed.

Julia's eyes widened and her heart leapt.

Buffalo! The same dates she'd be there performing with the Philharmonic! How lucky was that?

She barely held back on the impulse to respond instantly. She desperately wanted to tell him where and what time to be there. And to plan for a very long night. Not just for his magical boy-toy capabilities, but also every bit as much and maybe even more, for a chance to hold each other and kiss each other, both passionately and sweetly. Never letting go.

She stopped herself. This was, after all, the first of two messages. Perhaps the second would be a crusher, a message that yanked the rug out from under her and tore her heart apart. Perhaps—*please God, no!*—he had reconsidered after remembering how she'd cast him aside and ordered him out of the hotel room. Perhaps he had decided that she wasn't worth the trouble.

She had been such a fool!

With unsteady hands, Julia clicked on the second message.

I won't pester you if you aren't interested. I'm no stalker. I won't deluge you with messages if you tell me to stop. After this one, I'll wait at least a few weeks then give you the next month's locations on my travelling schedule. And if you tell me to never send you another message, I'll honor that with sadness (if you don't block my messages first).

As I said in my previous message, we'll play by your rules if we meet again. I'll keep my big mouth shut.

We had a lot of fun. We fit together nicely and not just in a boy-parts-in-a-girl-parts way. Haha. Although that was pretty spectacular, too.

What have you got to lose?

Slavko

Julia gasped, realizing she'd been holding her breath, eyes wide. Her heart hammered inside her chest. She licked her dry lips.

What did she have to lose? Nothing!

Nothing but the darkness that had enveloped her soul since she threw Slavko out of that hotel room.

"Yes!" Julia yelped and threw her hands into the air. "Yes! Yes! Yes!"

She double-checked the schedule on her phone, verified the hotel she'd be staying at in Buffalo, found another one nearby, and made a reservation for a room there.

And not just for one night. She typed her reply.

Slavko,

I would love to meet in Buffalo. I hated the way we parted in Boston. Hated it because we had such good times. You were such an amazing lover and after just our three nights together I knew you were a unique man.

I agree we had something special. Not happily-ever-after special. That can never happen so please do not use the L word no matter how wonderful we are making each other feel. Nor will I tell you my name, not even just my first name even though I know yours. I hope you understand that privacy and secrecy mean everything to me. If you can honor this need, as you have promised, we can enjoy a wonderful reunion.

If you can make it at our designated time after midnight on Friday night (actually very early Saturday morning), Saturday, and Sunday (actually Monday morning), that would be wonderful. I'll let you know the hotel and room number. Please let me know if all three evenings will work for you or if you will need Saturday night off to recuperate and restore your stamina. Haha. Not that you ever had an issue with that!

My heart and girl parts long for you, my dear Slavko. I look forward to wearing you out. Haha. But not just those magical lips and tongue and man parts of yours. I want all of you.

More than a week feels like an eternity to wait.

Your secret, special lover

All that remained was to hit the "Send Message" icon. Julia reread the message. She supposed she could fuss a bit more with the wording and try to make it perfect, but it was about as good as she could make it. She only regretted that one section: *Not happily-ever-after special. That can never happen so please do not use the L word no matter how wonderful we are making each other feel.*

She wished she could erase all of those words. She wished a happily ever after did await her.

A happily ever after with Slavko.

Julia blinked in shock. What was she thinking? Where had that come from? It was fine to secretly long for a happily ever after even though she knew it would destroy her musical career. And she might have fallen ass over teakettle for her dear Slavko. But to connect those two sticks of dynamite together, even if just in her mind for only a fleeting second, was to invite disaster.

She glanced at the message she'd written for herself earlier on the memo pad in the upper right corner of the desk.

Slavko is the Serpent!
Slavko is the Serpent!
Slavko is the Serpent!

She knew she was flirting with danger just to meet with Slavko again. Flirting with the Serpent! And for a fourth time! And if he really was available all three nights, then it would be a fourth, fifth, and sixth time with him!

Was she crazy? And then thinking impossible, unattainable thoughts like *A happily ever after with Slavko.* Was she nuts? She was!

She was inviting the Serpent into her Garden of Eden just because without him it didn't feel like a Garden of Eden anymore.

Without him it didn't feel like a Garden of Eden anymore.

Julia shrieked inwardly. Had she actually thought that? Yes, she had!

And it was true!

Slavko was the most dangerous man in the world. He could ruin her as totally as Xiangyu Lee had. And this time she would never recover.

She should delete the message right now. Before she sent it and risked everything just for a man.

She should delete it. Because *Slavko was the Serpent*!

Delete the message! Now! Before it's too late!

But she wanted Slavko! She wanted the Serpent! She needed the Serpent!

She loved Slavko!

"*No!*" What was she thinking? "*No! No! No!*"

"Slavko!" she said aloud, choking back a sob. "Slavko!"

Her hand trembled as her finger hovered over first the "Delete

Message" icon and then the "Send Message" icon. It swung back and forth. Delete. Send. Delete. Send. Back and forth. Back and forth.

Until finally, Julia shouted, "I want Slavko!" and pressed "Send Message."

When seconds later her phone rang, Julia shrieked, almost shooting out of her chair up through the ceiling. For a brief instant, she felt like a character in a Stephen King novel supernaturally communicated with by the object of her desires.

Then she saw the caller ID and belatedly recognized the ring tone. It wasn't Slavko, supernaturally summoned by her longing for him. And she wasn't going crazy. Just jittery and on edge.

Her heart rate, which had momentarily shot through the roof, plummeted. The beads of sweat that had begun their first stages of forming on her forehead cooled. Julia breathed a sigh of relief.

Then a different kind of anxiety took over. The call was from her mother.

Julia hadn't needed the caller ID that simply read "Mother" on the phone's screen to know she was returning Julia's call. Julia had given her mother her own ring tone, a fragment of the famous aria from Mozart's opera *The Magic Flute*, an aria sometimes associated in segments of pop culture with a shrewish, almost shrieking character—Mozart's mother-in-law in the movie *Amadeus* being a classic example—but assigned by Julia to her mother because the aria was one of the most technically difficult to perform in the repertoire. Her mother, after all, was the *prima donna* soprano for the Boston Opera Society, so the ring tone was a complement, not an association of her with a shrieking character.

At least that's how Julia explained it when her mother inadvertently butt-dialed one time while they were together. It was also how Julia felt about her almost half the time. She could perhaps even push the needle to fifty percent if she really worked at it.

But the truth was that her mother had always been a tough taskmaster and proud of it. Pushing Julia harder and harder almost from the instant she first picked up the violin. No matter how hard she practiced and no matter how quickly she reached prodigy stature, someone already famous like Sarah Chang was always far ahead. Nothing Julia did was quite good enough.

Forever A-minus.

That's how Julia still thought of those days before she finally escaped to the conservatory and then off on her own. Out of her mother's clutches. Julia could never cut her mother off like she'd been forced to do with her jealous former classmates turned toxic. One never cut off a parent. Ever. Julia remained the dutiful daughter, honoring her mother and her mostly silent father, wondering if one of them would ever repeat the words of pride in her achievements she'd heard that they expressed to their friends but never shared with her.

Julia wasn't holding her breath on that one.

She wished she could ignore this call and simply revel in thoughts of her upcoming nights with Slavko—*three wonderful nights!*—but knew she couldn't. The shrieking ring tone had set off a shriek of her own, terminating the glow of anticipation that had just begun to send its warmth all through her.

There was no getting that glow back now.

In fact, it almost felt as though her mother was calling to condemn her for her message to Slavko. The timing was a coincidence, of course. Julia didn't really believe in supernaturally based phone calls. But it felt beyond spooky that her finger had barely lifted from the "Send Message" icon when *The Magic Flute* high-pitched shriek erupted.

Her mother would, of course, hate everything about Slavko. Not just the shocking decadence of their lovemaking—images no mother ever wanted to see of her daughter—or that he wasn't Chinese. She would be appalled that Julia had allowed the Serpent into her musical Garden of Eden, a garden created in part by her mother's firm hand, stern direction, and uncompromising demands.

And Julia hadn't just *allowed* the Serpent in. She had *invited* him in knowing what he was, knowing how he could ruin her.

Could ruin her? *Would* ruin her.

And had rejoiced at the upcoming dalliance. Dancing on what would undoubtedly be her own musical grave.

"Hello, Mother," Julia said in the most casual tone she could manage.

A torturous silence hung in the air for what felt like an eternity.

"I was surprised to hear from you, Julia," her mother said. "Is everything all right?"

Julia could all but see her mother's frown and pursed lips of disapproval. She could all but feel the piercing eyes trying to peer inside her soul and discover her secrets.

"Yes, everything is fine," Julia said, belatedly trying to think of a cover story for why she had called hours earlier but coming up blank. "I just...I just figured it was a good time to talk to you."

"Oh," her mother said in a tone that conveyed she didn't believe a word of what Julia was saying. And who could blame her? Julia couldn't recall the last time she'd called her mother outside of their designated Monday time slot, etched into both of their calendars like a trip to the dentist.

"Are you sure you're okay?" her mother asked. "You sounded...*different* in your voicemail. Off. I could almost hear your pulse racing over the phone."

Julia shook her head, glad they were only using audio, not FaceTime. She couldn't conceal her moods, and quite scarily even some of her thoughts, from her mother.

"No, I was just..." Julia fumbled for words. Why hadn't she constructed a cover story when she had the chance? Because her subconscious had known she'd never pull it off? "I was just...it's just at the very beginning of the tour and I guess it feels like...oh, I don't know."

One hell of a cover story, Julia thought, and shook her head again.

"What's the problem?" her mother asked. "This isn't your first tour. It shouldn't be intimidating or feel overwhelming."

"It isn't that," Julia said. "Actually, I'm not sure what it is."

Of course, she knew exactly what it was. It had been a dark cloud hovering over her ever since she'd kicked Slavko out of that hotel room. A cloud that had grown thick and dark, thicker and ever darker until suddenly it had begun to part the instant she saw Slavko's first message. Brilliant sunlight had broken through. Warm and glowing...until that cloud reformed, thickened, and grew impenetrably dark when she considered deleting her massage to him, considering banishing Slavko, her Serpent, forever from her Garden of Eden.

But when she pressed send, the most perfectly brilliant sunlight burst through and blew away every last trace of the dark cloud. Julia's sky was the most beautiful, unclouded blue for the brief seconds until her mother's *The Magic Flute* high-pitched notes shattered that bliss.

"Did you get a bad review?" her mother asked.

"Oh, no. They've all been wonderful. At least the ones I've seen," Julia said, and forced a laugh. "Although I've forbidden Lisa from showing me any bad ones."

Julia winced. Why had she said that? Why admit anything to her mother, even a harmless truth like that?

Sure enough, Mother pounced like a wolf on raw meat.

"How can you improve if you shut off everything but blind praise? If a critic tells the truth but it's one you don't want to hear, you should still listen. Do you think you got this far by me telling you in your youth that every note you played was perfect?"

Blind praise. Her mother had actually used that phrase. As if any praise she received wasn't informed and artistically correct. As if the venomous critics of past years had told the truth when they inferred or outright stated that the great Julia Chu had reached the heights of her profession by sleeping her way to the top. Or at least providing better "eye candy," as one of them had put it, than her competitors.

"Ninety-nine out of every hundred critics are just bitter, failed artists," Julia snapped. "They'd be doing what I'm doing if they had the talent, the work ethic, and paid the dues I've paid! They wouldn't notice all but the most egregious artistic misstep unless it kicked them in the balls!"

Her mother gasped.

Julia closed her eyes and shook her head. How had she let Mother bait her like that? Why had she ever called her in the first place? Even if she'd lost every last shoulder to cry on and every sympathetic ear to listen, dead silence and toughing it out alone was better than this. She'd been toughing it out alone in dead silence for years.

Toughing it out alone and dead silence had been her best of friends.

"Well!" her mother muttered. "I never thought I'd hear my daughter talk to me that way."

"Mother, I'm sorry," Julia said, her eyes clenched shut as tears pooled in her eyes. "I didn't mean to snap at you."

"Well you certainly did!"

Silently, Julia mouthed the words: *Maybe I did mean to snap. Maybe I need to snap a little more. Maybe that would stop you from running over me like a bulldozer.*

"Did you just say something?" her mother asked with an edge in her voice.

Julia opened wide her eyes, held out her phone at arm's length, and stared at it. Had her mother's sometimes spooky powers over her been able to detect her silent mouthing out of words? Surely, that was paranoia. It must have been the soft exhalation of air as she mouthed the words. Perhaps in her anger the exhalation had not been so soft and the brushing of air over the phone's microphone had been enough to raise her mother's suspicions. Better to believe that than that her mother could somehow read her mind.

"No, I didn't say anything," Julia said. "And actually, I've got a call coming in that I have to take. I'm sorry I bothered you and sorry I snapped at you. I'll call you next Monday."

The words were met with stony silence.

Julia gave it five seconds, then said, "Goodbye, mother. I've got to go."

Chapter Sixteen

Slavko could no more contain his euphoria than he could go without oxygen. He didn't care if Happy Eddie or anyone else saw it. He didn't care if the rest of the world saw it and thought he was wearing the stupidest, most massive smile in the Universe.

Slavko...did...not...care.

He and Julia were getting together again! For three nights! *Three nights!* It boggled the mind!

Trying to compose himself at least a little, he left the restroom to which he'd excused himself when the ping came in on his phone. He hadn't noticed a thing about the restroom while he read Julia's message. It could have been in Siberia, Bermuda, or outer space for all he knew. With a spring in his step, Slavko stepped inside the closet-sized backstage dressing room where the boys were huddled, ready to go on stage.

The damp room, illuminated by a single light bulb hanging from a ceiling made of crumbling plaster, smelled of mold. Slavko did not care. There was barely enough room for the four of them to turn sideways without delivering or getting an elbow to the ribs. Slavko did not care. And it was almost cold enough to get their teeth to chattering. Slavko did not care.

Julia! Three nights!

"All set, boys?" he asked, trying to conceal his euphoria but knowing there was no hiding it.

"Man, whatever you got," Happy Eddie said, "you ought to bottle it. I'd guzzle a six-pack right now."

Slavko couldn't argue with the sentiment, but the joy he felt could not be bottled and was not for sale. It was attainable only for the luckiest guy in the world who was head over heels in love with Julia and knew that three nights of bliss awaited him.

"Sorry, big man," Slavko said. "Not for sale."

"Does Boston know?" Happy Eddie asked.

Slavko blinked, unsure what that was supposed to mean.

"What?" he asked.

Happy Eddie burst out laughing. "Ten minutes ago, you were as tense as a rattler ready to strike. I thought you were going to haul off and hit me back up there on the stage. Now, you're all sunshine and roses. Walking on air with the biggest, doofiest, dorkiest smile I've ever seen on you. And I've seen almost all your dorky smiles for the last twenty-five years.

"So unless you somehow got a quickie while we were waiting here, I figure that call you've being waiting for, checking your phone every two minutes, getting tenser and tenser, more and more wound up till you're damned near ready to snap, came in. Some honey you've been trying to reach here in Schenectady or maybe over in Albany finally got back to you. And you're just busting at the seams. Just makes me wonder if the Boston chi—the Boston gal—knows about this Schenectady honey."

Slavko laughed. Could he be any easier to read? Happy Eddie was wrong about there being two different women with whom he'd suddenly become a Romeo or a budding Don Juan, and was wrong about the meeting taking place in Schenectady or Albany this week. So no bull's-eye this time. But quite the near miss.

"Not exactly," Slavko said, still beaming. "But...you're not entirely wrong."

"Just tell us what's the night you're commandeering the Explorer so you can get your ashes hauled." Happy Eddie said.

"Next week in Buffalo," Slavko said. Not ready to break the news yet that it would be all three nights they were in the city, Slavko said, "Maybe more than just one night. But not just to, as you so eloquently put it, 'get my ashes hauled.'" He clapped his hands. "But enough of all that. Let's get out there and knock 'em dead!"

The Pied Piper Polish Polka Dots did in fact knock the audiences dead in all three performances that night and then again one night later. Six performances that were much-needed food for their artistic souls. All of them to packed, or near-packed, houses in the Kielbasa Korner bar. All of them with polka dancing up front close to the stage and appreciative applause. Raucous cheers following every accordion duel between Happy Eddie and Slavko. Not a heckler was to be found in a single one of the six crowds, many of whom included enthusiastic fans who stuck around for multiple shows.

It didn't get any better than that. It had been a joy to bound onto the stage with an extra spring in his step—Slavko guessed in all of their steps—and get the receptions they received.

And for Slavko, those three nights with Julia now confirmed were that much closer to reality. He was that much closer to heaven.

As the boys began carting the equipment out to the trailer, he headed to the bar owner's office up front to collect. Whistling idly, Slavko gave a smiling nod to the hulking, heavily tattooed bartender who looked more like a bouncer, and let his fingertips glide along the empty bar's polished surface. The pleasing smell of beer and kielbasa—nectar of the gods!— filled his nostrils.

Slavko knocked on the partially open door to the left of the front entrance and stepped inside. The owner, Clete something-or-other, sat behind a wooden desk stacked with papers. Bald with white hair around the sides, he had a doughy face and dark-rimmed glasses that had slid partway down his bulbous nose.

"Nice job out there," Clete said, handing Slavko a modestly thick white business envelope. "We'll have to get you back out here again."

"Thank you," Slavko said. "We had a great time. So did the audiences, I'm quite sure."

He opened the unsealed envelope and began counting the cash. In the old days, he'd instinctively taken the offered envelopes and counted the money in private. His upbringing had taught him to trust people. Counting cash to verify the amount was the worst of manners. It simply was not done.

But it didn't take many venues on the road to teach him a much different lesson. Trust no one but your family and the closest of friends. Strangers could not be trusted and bar owners were the worst of all.

Slavko's heart, filled with jubilation an instant earlier, sank. He felt sick to his stomach, as if he'd been gut-punched.

He looked up and stared at the bar owner, who had crossed his arms and leaned back in his chair, jaw set.

"This isn't the amount we agreed to," Slavko said, his entire being filling with fury.

"I'll need you to sign a receipt," the owner said, ignoring him.

"This is barely half of what we agreed to!" Slavko shouted. His hands and voice shook with rage as he counted the bills again. "We had a contract! A flat rate and a percentage of the take beyond the specified minimum! Six performances! And almost all of them to a full house! There wasn't a single person in the audience that wasn't drinking your beer and most of them were eating your goddamned kielbasa. You're screwing us!"

Simultaneously, Happy Eddie and the hulking bartender appeared over Slavko's shoulder. The bartender stood six-five and looked like an NFL linebacker with a shaved head, an enormous, chiseled chest, and thick, heavily tattooed arms. He held a sawed-off baseball bat in one hand and slapped it against the other massive palm.

"Is there a problem?" the brute asked in a tone that made the question rhetorical, a tone that said there was no problem at all and Slavko could kindly get the hell out of there or be thrown out, or if he so preferred, beaten half to death. Happy Eddie, wide-eyed and frozen, appeared ready to shit his pants.

"Yes, there's a problem!" Slavko snapped, spinning back around to face the owner, leaving the behemoth uncomfortably out of sight. If the goon was going to hit him over the head, hopefully Happy Eddie would break out of his trance early enough to shout a warning. "We had a contract for six performances and we fulfilled that contract to the letter and then some! We are not going to be cheated!"

"Most of your audience were our regular customers," the owner said calmly, as if talking to a child. "You don't get a cut of the take off our regular customers. We'd be giving money away."

"That's bullshit and you know it!" Slavko snapped. "You can't tell me that when we packed the house for six shows all of them were your regular customers. More importantly, that isn't what the contract says!"

The owner smiled benevolently. "Oh, I'm sure it's in the fine print somewhere. Perhaps you'd like to take this to Judge Judy."

Slavko felt his face flush. The top of his head seemed ready to explode like a volcano. He'd read the entire contract. There was no fine print that he'd missed.

The mocking jab about Judge Judy infuriated Slavko even more. The owner knew full well that Slavko's chances of taking him to small claims court and showing up for the appearance—driving all the way from wherever they were on that date—were close to zero. It was every bar owner's "I can screw you and get away with it" loophole.

"You want me to take care of this myself, boss?" the behemoth behind Slavko asked, slapping the sawed-off bat against his palm again. "Or shall I call our cops?"

Our cops. Slavko knew what that meant, too. The local police or even private security. Between that and a friendly judge in small claims court amounted to what sports teams would call an insurmountable home field advantage.

The usually pleasing aroma of kielbasa and beer suddenly threated to make Slavko sick. He hoped he never smelled that shit ever again.

"Let's go, Slavko," Happy Eddie said with a tremor in his voice.

The owner held out a ledger and pen, a gleam in his eyes and a victorious smirk on his lips.

"Sign the receipt or give me back the money," he said. "Unless you'd like to become acquainted with a Louisville Slugger."

Chapter Seventeen

Julia strode onto the Kimmel Center for the Performing Arts stage, beaming her most brilliant smile. She held the priceless Stradivarius and bow in her left hand while the fingertips of her right lifted the hem of her elegant floor-length, strapless, bright blue gown ever so slightly to avoid any possibility of tripping. Enthusiastic applause from the audience—every seat filled from the main floor to the three balconies—washed over her. The members of the Philadelphia Orchestra, the men all wearing the traditional black tuxedoes with white ties and the women equally conservative black dresses, stood as she moved past them. The bespectacled conductor, Wilhelm Schmidt, bald but with gray hair around the sides and a matching, neatly trimmed beard, followed in her wake, reached behind her to shake the concertmaster's hand, then took her hand as they faced the audience and she gave a slight bow.

The Kimmel Center was one of her favorite venues. Shaped like the curving body of a cello, its very design spoke to the beauty and seriousness of the music played within its walls. It looked spectacular with its dark mahogany surfaces and ceilings to each tier. Its acoustics sounded even better.

Julia hoped to follow suit, beginning with the beauty and elegance of her own appearance. Her long black hair was pulled back and held in place by her favorite three-stone jade hairclip. Her necklace and earrings were similarly made of gold-encircled jade. She always wore jade jewelry when performing, paying tribute to her Chinese heritage while also following the protocol of avoiding the distraction of glittering diamonds. Her strapless, bright blue gown was also one of her favorites, even if it provided possible confirmation to her jealous critics who contended her success was fueled mostly by her beauty. To hell with them, she thought, and bless the trailblazer who established decades ago that soloists, especially female ones, could and should wear beautiful and possibly even flamboyant clothing while everyone else on stage remained stodgily in black and white.

Even more importantly, though, Julia sought to bring the most beautiful sound out of her priceless Stradivarius to more than match the acoustics of the Kimmel Center. Looks were superficial; the magnificence of the Sibelius Violin Concerto, sublime. It was a piece that was not only one of the two or three most technically demanding in the repertoire: it also spoke to the soul.

Julia nodded to the conductor and prepared for the *allegro moderato*.

Everything was perfect in this Garden of Eden. Everything. Everything had been perfect ever since she had reconnected with Slavko. Though he was only in the very deepest recesses of her being at this moment—her mind and soul totally focused on the Sibelius—her messages with him since their reconnection had filled the emptiness deep within her.

It had even kept her going, smiling—at least most of the time—during Monday's interrogation, disguised as conversation, by her mother.

"Are you doing better today than last week?" her mother asked.

"I'm fine," Julia said. "Things are going great."

"That's good to hear. You sounded out of sorts last time we talked."

"I'm fine."

"You even snapped at me."

Still clinging to that like a dog to its bone? Julia rolled her eyes and shook her head. "I apologized for that, Mother. Was there a need to bring it up again?"

"It was just that you were quite disrespectful."

"I was disrespectful toward critics, not toward you," Julia said, mentally adding that her mother had in so many ways been her harshest critic. Other than herself, of course. "I only used colorful language to make that point and for that I did apologize."

"Fine." Julia could all but see her mother's pursed lips and disapproving eyes that had not truly accepted any apology. "I just wonder, Julia, if you get too lonely on these tours."

Julia smiled and felt a warm glow at the thought of Slavko. He cleansed all sense of loneliness when he was with her, although she could only imagine how aghast her mother would be at even the very idea of her and Slavko in the bedroom, much less the salacious details. Julia almost burst out laughing at that thought.

"I'm not lonely," Julia said.

Not anymore.

"You do know that I would join you for a part of the tour if my schedule allowed it."

Julia shuddered at the thought.

"Of course, and I appreciate that," Julia said, because those words were expected.

"I do hope that one of these days you'll meet someone, perhaps on this tour."

Oh yes, I have, Julia thought, and took in a deep breath. Someone wonderful and not just in superficial matters. It was, of course, absurd to think she knew all about Slavko. She knew next to nothing about him. But in just their three nights together, she thought she had glimpsed into his soul and seen a beauty beyond that of his mere good looks and on par with his amazing lovemaking.

It might be presumptuous—in fact, she was certain that it was presumptuous—to believe she'd gained that much insight into Slavko's heart in just three nights, much less three nights spent almost exclusively in blissful, orgasmic coupling. But there it was. There was no convincing her otherwise.

He was the kind of man who could make her very happy for—

Julia jerked back from that cliff. What was she thinking?

"What did you say, dear?" her mother asked.

"I didn't say anything. I didn't want to interrupt."

And on the topic of her meeting a man, her mother never stopped at just one sentence.

"Oh, I thought you said something. Or gasped. Or something."

Perhaps she had gasped, Julia thought, at least a little when she got thinking about how happy Slavko could make her and how far she was taking that thought.

Waaaay too far.

"No," Julia said, getting her mind back on track.

"It just seems that you come in contact with so many musicians and other people associated with music. People of a like mind. Surely there should be a man you find interesting."

Oh yes. So *very* interesting.

"A Chinese man, of course," her mother added, stating the obvious. "That narrows the possibilities, but I wonder if you just aren't looking hard enough. Or your expectations are too high. You know, you aren't getting any younger."

And there it was. The iceberg lurking beneath the surface of her mother's arctic ocean. It wasn't enough that Julia had ascended to the absolute pinnacle of solo violinists, on par with even the great Itzhak Perlman and Sarah Chang. No, she also needed to pop out grandchildren for her not-so-patient mother. As the only child, that burden fell exclusively on her. And at the nightmarishly advanced age of twenty-nine—practically at death's door—her biological clock was reaching doomsday.

"Mother, we've talked about this before," Julia says. "It'll happen when it happens." For the first time, she added, "If it's supposed to happen."

Her mother gasped.

"Well, of course it's supposed to happen!"

Chapter Eighteen

A blast of warm air from the Explorer's vents yanked Slavko from his restless sleep. Groggily, he lifted his head off the pillow crammed against the door frame and side window. He peered through the fogged-up windshield at the overhead glow of the Motel 6 parking lot's sodium lights. They'd been parked for most of the night in the lot, halfway to Buffalo, trying to sleep but freezing their asses off. Like clockwork every couple hours, Happy Eddie had started the engine and fired up the heat until the cabin was sufficiently warm, or at least no longer bitterly cold, then turned it off again and went back to snoring like a chain saw.

The smell of stale sweat, onions, and garlic filled the heavy air. Slavko pulled his thick wool blanket up to his chin and adjusted the pillow against the cold window. His seat was reclined a quarter of the way back, better than trying to sleep with it fully upright but a far cry from lying horizontally and a million miles from the comfort of a warm bed. Every muscle in his body felt cramped. He longed to stretch his legs out to full extension, but even with his feet firmly pressed up against the footwell's front wall, his knees remained bent at a forty-five degree angle. Though he was a shade under six feet tall, he felt like an NBA seven-footer whose cramped legs all but pressed up against his chest.

Too broke even for Motel 6. The band's fortunes in a nutshell. How headshakingly bad was that? Might make a good title for a country song, Slavko thought, but it felt more like a funeral dirge for the Pied Piper Polish Polka Dots.

After getting stiffed by the Kielbasa Korner Bar owner, the band had at least gotten what they'd been promised for their weekend gig in Albany, but that had been no lucrative windfall. So with a couple nights off before their performances in Buffalo—Slavko had struck out in his long shot attempts at last-minute bookings—this marked the much-needed opportunity to save a few night's hotel bills. Put up with the discomfort of sleeping in the Explorer and the smell of everyone two days removed from their last shower. Keep the ship afloat. There'd be plenty of time to take extra-long, extra-hot showers to look presentable and feel alive again in Buffalo. That was, of course, as long as they didn't rip each other's heads off in the meantime with the inevitable short tempers.

Too broke even for Motel 6. Slavko supposed it could be worse. Instead of October, it could be January, with temperatures so freezing cold it wouldn't be safe to brave nights slept in the Explorer even with Happy Eddie periodically getting the heater going.

Ah, the glamor of the road.

Slavko winced as he attempted to stretch his legs just a wee bit more—please, just a little more!—then in frustration, turned in his seat. What he wouldn't give to be sleeping in a warm bed right now.

Paying dues sucked. There were times that the band's art seemed like a loan shark who kept demanding his dues get paid over and over, and no matter how many payments were collected, it still didn't even pay the vig.

Slavko wasn't about to give up. You couldn't put a price on living your dream. But as he twisted to get a kink out of his thigh and behind him Junior loudly passed gas—no more Taco Bell for him—Slavko couldn't deny that at times the dream behaved like a nightmare.

And yet a warmth glowed inside him even while his nose, ears, and face tingled from the cold and his cramped muscles screamed for release. In just a few short days, he would again see Julia. And not for just one night. For three nights!

Her exquisite, petite body. Her beautiful face with its model's high cheekbones and flawless complexion. Her sparkling eyes. Her blindingly bright smile that could light up a room. The smell of her lavender perfume and the musky scent of her lovemaking. Her soft lips and their wintergreen taste. Her taste *down there*. Her exhilarating sexual appetite. Her husky voice issuing commands during sex. The caress of her fingertips. The exuberant eroticism of her moans or ecstatic orgasms.

But if they never even took their clothes off, just seeing her would be enough. He wanted Julia, of course. Wanted her sexually so much he could taste it. And he knew that when it came down to it, they wouldn't be able to keep their hands off each other. But his desire went far beyond just the erotic. It went all the way to his soul.

He was head over heels in love with Julia in a way totally unlike he'd ever felt for a woman, even Norma Mae.

Was that even possible after just three nights? That was crazy. Insane. Impossible. Any yet wasn't everything about Julia and him together crazy, insane, and impossible?

Crazy wonderful. Insane glorious. Impossible happiness.

Just four days away. In some ways that felt like an eternity, but at the same time it was also so close he could taste it. Four days! That equated to...ninety-six hours. He approximated the mental calculation and came up with five or six thousand minutes.

Five or six thousand minutes until he once again saw Julia.

Tick...tick...tick...

Chapter Nineteen

Julia sat on the edge of the hotel room's king-size bed, one with a dark gray upholstered headboard, waiting impatiently. She was dressed in a satin, bronze-colored negligee with matching panties straight from Victoria's Secret. She'd dabbed lavender perfume on her neck, wrists, between her breasts, and on the inside of her thighs. Had chewed a wintergreen Certs. Had donned only the most obvious parts of her disguise—the flowing, rust-colored wig and the librarian's black-rimmed glasses—but had ditched the bright red lipstick, the heavy shades of eye shadow, and the contact lenses that turned her soft brown eyes to brightest blue.

The standard-issue, moderately-upscale room had a small, white-painted wooden desk and dresser up against the wall she faced, a TV mounted above the dresser, and a refrigerator to the side, a coffee maker atop it. To her left, the drapes were closed across the half-height window.

Slavko was due in just three minutes. Julia was jumping out of her skin with anticipation. She could...not...wait.

The nine days had felt like forever. She had even considered summoning Slavko a day earlier since he'd indicated he'd be in the city by Thursday night. But that would have been not only ushering her Serpent into the Garden of her music, it would have been inviting the Serpent to burn the place down until her career was nothing but ashes.

With only the one exception of Thursday nights, she and Slavko could frolic for as many hours as their bodies allowed and she could sleep in, get a good night's rest, and still have hours and hours left for practice the next day. There would be no compromise to her artistry. On Thursdays throughout this tour, however, Julia would practice with the orchestra for the first time, followed by a Friday morning dress rehearsal and the first performance that evening.

As a result, Thursday nights were sacred. She and Slavko couldn't have their fun until three in the morning or later and still allow her to get sufficient rest before the morning's dress rehearsal. If she crossed that line, it would only a matter of time before her career slipped or even cratered. Rock stars might be able to abuse their bodies in that way and still get away with it. A violin soloist wouldn't stand a chance. A piece as demanding as the Sibelius or the Tchaikovsky, initially deemed to be unplayable because of its difficulty, would crush her.

So Julia had honored her commitment to her art by holding off on a Thursday night invitation to Slavko, much as she'd been tempted, and that restraint had been rewarded, at least artistically, with this evening's flawless performance of the Tchaikovsky. It had left her beaming to the adoring crowd and beaming inwardly to herself. She had loved everything about the performance.

She'd paid the price of waiting for Slavko one more night, but now intended to collect fully on that investment.

She was *ready*. But not just *down there*. She was very much ready *down there*, but she also felt a longing in her heart just to see him again.

She was ready *all over*.

Slavko's knock came precisely on time, so precise that Julia wondered if he'd waited in the hallway until his watch showed the exact prescribed minute. Never a minute early or late.

She dashed to the hotel room door, so eager that she almost flung the door open before checking the peephole. Almost. The dangers, of course, only began with paparazzi. She'd encountered them only twice in her career, but wouldn't one of those vermin love to take pictures of her standing there in her revealing negligee? The tabloid headline would most certainly include the words "love nest." And of course, the possibilities grew infinitely more dangerous from there. Every woman had to beware. So Julia performed her due diligence and scanned the peephole. She squealed with the delight of a little schoolgirl when she saw Slavko.

She stepped behind the door, opened it for him to enter, and launched herself at him, wrapping her arms around his neck and smothering him with a succession of long, passionate kisses. She breathed in the scent of cedarwood with a slight hint of nutmeg and citrus. Tasted the mint on his lips. Clung to him as he held her tight with a single arm around her waist.

It was heaven to be in his arms again, kissing those soft lips, feeling his body against hers. She wanted the kisses never to end. When she finally came up for air, she led Slavko to the bed where her euphoria grew ever greater.

She all but tore off his clothes. She did, in fact, pop two buttons on his blue dress shirt, worn with black dress jeans that she quickly flung to the floor.

She lay atop him on the bed, kissing his soft lips, running her hands through his thick, dark, wavy hair. His hands caressed her breasts through the satin, bronze-colored negligee, thumbing her nipples until they were hard. Then his hands roamed to her panties where he stroked her butt cheeks. She felt the length of his hardness up against her crotch. She leaned back and wriggled and rubbed against it.

Pleasure poured through her entire body. But especially down there. It felt *sooooo* good.

She wanted him inside her. All of him. But she wanted his amazing mouth and lips first. Wanted them kissing and tonguing and devouring her *down there.*

She slid up his body, intending to straddle his head, then lower herself down upon his face as she had done before. Let him pleasure her with his magical mouth and tongue until she could gasp in ecstasy no longer, using the amazing lung capacity befitting his barrel chest that allowed him to service her while a mere mortal would be gasping for air.

Julia wanted that more than anything. Wanted it so badly her skin tingled all over. And she would get it.

She slid up his body until her breasts, still cloaked in the negligee, were in Slavko's face. He kissed her breasts through the silky fabric. Tongued her nipples.

She wriggled out of the negligee, pulling it over her head and tossing it aside so he could have direct access. The panties followed. The erotic scent of his cedarwood cologne filled her nostrils.

She moaned as he licked and sucked on her nipples. His hands caressed her butt cheeks. A hand slipped between her legs. A finger slid along her wetness. Rubbed her clit.

Julia gasped.

But what she wanted right then, right at that very instant, was his mouth and tongue working their magic on her down there. Not his finger, which felt wonderful and was bringing her close to the brink in just seconds. Nor his cock or anything else.

His mouth and tongue on her. She had to have it. Have it *now*.

Now!

She straightened up. Pulled the pillow out from beneath Slavko's head and tossed it aside.

Now!

She grasped the dark gray upholstered headboard, barely sensing its smooth texture, and moved upward astride Slavko's body.

Now!

Swung one bent leg to the side of his head. Had to have him. Had to have him *now*. His mouth. His tongue.

Now!

Swung the other leg up to plant it beside Slavko's other ear. Lowered herself onto his warm lips.

And moaned as Slavko nibbled and kissed and licked and sucked. Nibbled and kissed. Licked and sucked. It felt...amazing!

Slavko devoured her.

The orgasms flooded over Julia. They exploded in her mind. They exploded *down there.* They exploded all over.

She gasped with desire. She gasped for breath. She squeezed tight her grip on the headboard as she began to feel dizzy. Her hips squeezed harder down on Slavko's mouth.

Oh...my...God!

And when she thought the oral orgiastic insanity could get no more mind-blowing, Julia for the first time considered reciprocating. The thought had never occurred to her with Slavko. She'd gone down on a man only once and found it distasteful, the brute saying vile things and even slapping her face—"just playing around," he'd tried to explain later—making it feel degrading and disgusting. She'd never again performed the act, no matter how much the man pleaded and complained that her desire for oral pleasure made it a one-way street. Tough shit. With her other lovers—not that many, really, but all discreet, one-night stands, never to meet again, avoiding all messy emotional entanglements—she hadn't really cared.

But this was Slavko. Slavko was different.

And so as one wave of orgasms ended and before another could wash her away, she crawled off Slavko's face, turned around and saw his beautiful hardness at full readiness for her to return the favor. He had not yet put on a condom. She hesitated for a second, not wanting to risk another bad experience in the act and spoil this magical night with this magical man.

But she wanted to give Slavko as much pleasure as possible. Not just take and take and take, though he'd certainly been delighted and had commented that his nights with her had been the best of his life. She'd given an abundance of pleasure even as she'd captained the ship of their desires and had guided it according to her own erotic radar.

But she wanted more for him.

And so she bent down and put her mouth on his hardness. Slavko groaned with pleasure. And because it was Slavko, she groaned with pleasure, too. She'd never, ever thought she could enjoy this.

But she did.

Slavko was different. Slavko changed everything.

And when he said, "Let me take care of you, too," grabbed a pillow and shoved it behind his head, then guided her legs and hips to straddle him again so they could pleasure each other orally at the same time, she loved him all the more.

Loved him all the more.

She froze for an instant as the words formed in her mind and soul even though not spoken aloud—*what was she thinking? No L word!*—but hadn't that ship sailed within her mind long ago? And then that magical mouth and tongue of his began licking and kissing and sucking her clit and all conscious thought left her, was simply not possible, as the tsunami of pleasure washed over her and drowned her in a torrent of ecstasy.

With the salty taste of Slavko's ejaculate lingering in her mouth, shockingly not unpleasant, Julia slipped a condom on his still-unflagging erection and mounted him.

Going down on a man. And *enjoying* it. Who would have thought? And then sweet sixty-nine. Even better. And finally feeling strangely pleased, as opposed to disgusted, at the salty taste still in her mouth.

Was everything pleasing with Slavko?

She loved the feeling of him now deep inside of her. Deep all the way. And then out. In. Out. Pausing that motion briefly with him deep inside her to grind against him, moving ever so slightly back and forth. Then back to in and out, in and out, in deep all the way. And out.

Sometimes with Slavko's thumb caressing her clit. Sometimes her own middle finger playing with it. Sometimes both.

It was all good. All great.

Sometimes with her sitting upright atop him as she moved. Often with her back arched in pleasure as the ecstasy coursed through her system, making her skin tingle. Sometimes with Slavko caressing her small breasts, thumbing the nipples. Sometimes caressing the curve of her sides or her butt. And of course her clit.

It was all good. All great.

Other times, she bent over so she could wrap her arms around his neck even as she moved up and down. Smothered him with kisses on his soft lips, some short and sweet, some long and passionate, lasting until she had to pull away just to breathe.

All good. All great.

Their bodies lovingly intertwined, their moans of passion shared.

All good. All great.

Hours to ride before I sleep. The phrase popped into her head from God knew where. She guessed it came from some old half-remembered poem or was a butchered version of that poem. Who cared? It matched how she felt.

Hours to ride before I sleep.

They were just getting started. She couldn't get enough of this man. She kissed him hungrily. Lovingly. Devouring his lips as fully as he had devoured her *down there*. And, she supposed, as fully as she had shockingly devoured his cock. Only in the deepest recesses of her mind did she notice that the taste of his lips and mouth bore traces of her own juices from his oral magic on her.

It was all good. All great.

Her only focus was on this wonderful man. *Slavko.* She ran her fingers through his thick hair. Kissed him even more deeply. Luxuriated in the pleasure of him inside her. Filling her.

Hours to ride before I sleep. Oh yes, hours to ride before I sleep.

She stopped.

But what does Slavko *want? Not what do* I *want. What does* he *want?*

She blinked. Slavko caressed her side. His hips moved beneath her.

Did she always have to be the captain of the ship of their desires? Wasn't it his turn?

A concerned look crossed Slavko's face. "What's wrong?"

"What do *you* want?" Julia asked.

"What do you mean?" he asked, confused. "I want what you want." And then, warily, "Is that a trick question?"

"Why would you say that?" Julia replied, wondering why he would ever consider it a trick question. But stopped wondering when she recalled her prohibition—one which her own mind too often ignored—that there could be no talk of love and forever and happily ever after. He'd started to speak of it in Boston and she'd thrown him out of her bed. And, for a time, out of her life. So of course he was afraid to say or do the wrong thing.

"I mean," she added, "do you want to be on top? Some other position? Something else? Tell me what you want."

Slavko beamed a sigh of relief.

"My greatest pleasure," he said, "is driving you wild with pleasure. Nothing gives me greater satisfaction."

That was a very, very, very good answer.

And when they could continue no more, Julia shocked Slavko and herself even more. They lay in each other's arms, feeling the ultimate in post-coital bliss. Bodies tight against each other. Caressing each other. Showering each other with both short and long, loving, passionate kisses.

The words popped out of her mouth before she realized it.

"Stay the night," she said.

Chapter Twenty

S lavko didn't think he had a snowball's chance in hell of falling asleep. How could he? The most amazing woman in the world lay beside him beneath the sheets and bedcovers, her beautiful face sideways on the pillow, her jet-black hair—minus the ridiculous rust-colored wig—arrayed behind her. The pleasing scents of their lovemaking and her lavender perfume lingered in his nostrils.

Together, they'd quickly determined they stood no chance of sleep if they remained naked and intertwined. They might be orgasmed out, but the sensual parts of their bodies seemed to take their bare skin and physical proximity as a challenge to perhaps go at it one more time even when impossible. Giggling at their plight, Julia had slipped her negligee back on and Slavko had stepped back into his shorts. Neither article of clothing acted as perfect passion stiflers, but it was the best they could do.

They lay facing each other initially, legs intertwined, a hand on the other's high hip. But though they couldn't see each other hardly at all in a darkness broken only by three soft nightlights placed ten feet apart at the base of the far wall, they could still feel each other's warm breath on their face and let their mind's eye fill in what the physical eye could not perceive.

Finally, Julia turned away. Slavko snuggled up to her within an inch or two of actual sleep-defeating contact with the satin negligee and looped his arm around her, his hand settling on the flat of her stomach.

He was the happiest man in the world. He was with the woman he loved, spending his first full night with her. Both of them exhausted from hours of lovemaking. Lovemaking that had never been better, even if Julia refused to even consider the L word. There had been the purely physical gratification, of course. An overflowing bounty of orgiastic pleasure. But if she were honest with herself, Julia would have to admit that the love she seemed to be running from was in full view between them. The passionate kisses. The caresses. The fondling. The holding tight and never wanting to let go.

That wasn't mere raw, animalistic sex. That was making love.

Making L-O-V-E. Love, love, love.

Love that pulsed from the depths of their hearts. His heart for sure. He knew it to the depths of his soul. And her heart, too, if she'd only admit it.

The best thing on Earth.

Lying here with the most wonderful woman in the world, Slavko wondered if he even dared to fall asleep. Did he dare risking that when he awoke Julia would no longer be lying next to him?

That he'd been gifted this time of Heaven on Earth and slept through it?

Slavko's mind climbed groggily up from the depths of deep sleep. Thin streams of sunlight broke through the darkness to stab him in the eyes. Where was he? What day was it? The tough, seemingly impossible questions of life on the road. He groaned.

His eyes shot open.

Julia! Was she—

He whirled in the bed and—

Julia lay there beside him, smiling brightly. She was still there. He had not slept through his gift of Heaven on Earth.

"Good morning, stranger," she said, her eyes sparkling in a way that should be impossible first thing in the morning. She moved close and kissed him.

More Heaven on Earth.

Slavko wrapped his arms around her and held her warm body close to his. He never wanted to let go. Heaven on Earth. He softly stroked her cheek.

"Julia, you are amazing!" he said.

Julia recoiled, eyes wide with fear. She pushed him away and jumped out of the bed as if it were on fire.

"What did you just say?" she asked, raw terror in her voice.

"I said you're amazing." Slavko said, not understanding what was wrong.

"No, that isn't what you said. You said, *'Julia,* you are amazing!' *Julia! Julia! Julia! How do you know my name?"*

Slavko's heart sank. All the air rushed out of his lungs. A groan escaped from his lips. He felt as though he'd been kicked in the nuts.

He stared at the raw fury and terror in Julia's eyes and didn't know what to say.

"How do you know my name?" Julia asked again in a near shriek. *"Answer me!"*

"I can explain," Slavko said, even though he really couldn't.

He sat up, trying to clear the cobwebs in his muddled mind, knowing with a brokenhearted certainty that he had lost her. This time for good.

His Heaven on Earth had truly lasted all of last night, and he'd slept through it. It had just ended when he opened his big mouth.

"What?" Julia demanded.

"I saw your picture in the paper," Slavko said, able to speak only the truth. Lies never worked. At least not for him. Never had. Even this lie of omission—as completely unavoidable as it might have been because it was the only way to see Julia again—was about to cost him the love of his life.

Was going to cost him everything.

"The picture was in *The Boston Globe,*" he continued. "I recognized you right away. Said your name was Julia Chu, but they called you *La*

Petite Rockette. I guess you're the next Itzhak Perlman. Or you already are. And you were starting a world tour."

Eyes suddenly bleak and without hope, Julia staggered backwards away from him. Her backside bumped into the wooden desk. She grasped onto the desk chair for support.

"I should have known it would come to this," she said. "I should have known better."

She spun the chair halfway around and sank into it. Crossed her arms on the back of the chair and buried her head in her arms.

Slavko bolted out of the bed and rushed to her side. He rested a hand on her shoulder.

"Everything will be fine," he said in as soothing a voice as he could muster.

Julia flung his hand away.

"Get out!" she commanded icily.

"We can keep what we have a secret, if that's what you want, if that's what you need," Slavko said, fumbling for the right words. "I would never betray you."

"Yeah, you're great at keeping a secret!" Julia said.

The words felt like a slap. Slavko knew he deserved them. He felt like killing himself for letting her name slip out like that. Of course, she couldn't trust him now.

"I joined that stupid website and got the app," she said, "because my privacy could never be broken. Never! I don't have the time and the energy for a conventional relationship, one that would play well in the media. All of my energies must go into my art. But sometimes even I get lonely.

"So I signed up as long as there was no chance of me being discovered. Not one chance of a lover ever knowing my name. I couldn't afford it. It would ruin me. Especially with the awful lies that were spread about me years ago.

"I suppose there was always a chance that a random lover would be a classical violin fan who recognized me, but what were the odds, especially with the disguise? But now I'm ruined. I'll be the slut they said I was."

She looked away and stared at the wall as if somehow the answer was written there. "I've only done this a handful of times. I guess it only took one."

"I won't say a word," Slavko said, promising again, almost adding the words "I love you!"

Words that had prompted his banishment just a few short weeks ago. Which gave him an idea.

"You told me after my big-mouthed mistake last time," he said, "that I could never again use the L word or speak of a real future for us and of course, no happily ever after. Did I live up to that...that requirement?"

He almost used the word "demand," only softening it to "requirement" at the last instant.

Julia said nothing.

"I never broke my promise," Slavko said, answering his own question. "Even at the height of our lovemaking when I"—Slavko hesitated, then decided to gamble all-in—"when I wanted to say the L word over and over, wanted to all but shout it from the rooftops because I feel so passionately about you. I did as you required because of my feelings for you.

"And because of the intensity of those feelings, I would never, ever, ever betray you. If you decide to kick me out that door right now and never see me again, I'll be heartbroken, but I will never betray you. Not to my best friends. Not to anyone. I'll take our secret to the grave, if it comes to that."

Julia nodded sadly.

"I believe you, my dear Slavko," she said. "I believe in your passionate words. And I want to believe you would never knowingly betray me and this dark secret. But my name slipped out of your mouth this morning. And I can't have you or anyone else blabbing my name anytime they're half asleep or half drunk or half stoned. Or maybe just plain angry. Couples have been known to fight, you know. One argument and next thing you know, the whole world hears about it. *TMZ. People* magazine. The *National Enquirer.*"

Slavko's heart started to break. Julia had made her decision and there was nothing he could say to change it. They were done. She'd given him this one more chance and he'd blown it.

He'd held Heaven on Earth in his hands, then pissed it away.

But dammit, he wasn't going to give up. Julia was worth fighting for. What they had together was worth fighting for.

So he would fight.

"Listen," Slavko said, trying to frame his argument on the fly. "If you think I would divulge your secret to anyone for any reason, even a bone-headed slip of the tongue, then that's true whether you kick me out the door forever or keep our next date tonight. I know your secret. I *am* your secret. You gain nothing by saying goodbye to me forever. You'll only break my heart and, I think, break your own heart, too."

Julia cupped her face in her hands and shook her head.

"I don't know what to do," she said. "I'm so confused. But I have to leave now and so do you. I'm sure you've got business to take care of here in Buffalo, and I have a concert tonight to prepare for." With a wry look, she added, "As you are well aware."

"Meet me tonight," Slavko said. "You have nothing to lose and everything to gain." He caressed her arm and felt buoyed that she didn't pull away. "We can just talk. Not even take a stitch of clothes off. Talk about this. Talk about anything *but* this. Talk about whatever you want. Do whatever you want. Whatever it takes for you to believe you can trust me."

Slavko had left the Explorer and trailer with the boys, not wanting to fray nerves by commandeering the vehicle all the time, so he needed an Uber ride to get back to their hotel. He hated the expense, but any cost to see Julia was worth it. He waited until he got outside the hotel to call for the ride, but the app he really wanted to hear from wasn't Uber. It was DiscreetPartnerForYou with a message from Julia. Perhaps that she'd decided and they were definitely on for that night. Or a request to return to the room. To answer a question. To reassure her that her secret was safe. To kill a spider, if it came to that.

Or for a kiss. For a long, loving hug. Good lord, maybe even another of her delightful bucking bronco rides if he was up to it.

Whatever she wanted. As long as she wanted him.

But there was nothing.

Chapter Twenty-One

It had been so perfect. Until it wasn't.

Back in her official hotel room, away from what the tabloid media would call her love nest if those jackals ever found out, Julia took the longest of long, hot showers to prepare for the day ahead. She still felt the frozen chill that had run up and down her back when she'd heard the word "Julia" escape from Slavko's lips.

Why had she ever thought she could keep her secret bottled up and hidden from the public? She was such a fool. Even with how little she used DiscreetPartnerForYou, wasn't it inevitable that eventually she'd be recognized and exposed? If not by a lover, then by a hotel clerk or even a random stranger in a hotel lobby, elevator, or hallway.

Her heart felt leaden. A lifetime of work and dedication to achieve her dreams about to go down the drain.

Possibly.

The ironic thing was that what DiscreetPartnerForYou offered—anonymous one-night stands to minimize the chance of discovery—was also what the public would consider most scandalous and what would cause the stuffed-shirt component of her audience to desert her. The tiniest chance of discovery but the greatest destruction. An affair with one of their own or even an acquaintance in a bar could be accepted. Internet sex with a stranger would not. At least not in a woman who'd barely fended off rumors that she'd slept her way to the top.

Her life was in Slavko's hands. Or at least her career was, which amounted to the same thing. Her career was her life.

So how could she have been so foolish? Why had she even needed a man in the first place? How could that little bit of loneliness ever been worth the risk? It made Julia sick to even think about it.

Compartmentalize. It was all that Julia could do. She had to quarantine this crisis into the deepest recesses of her mind and not let it infect her art. She could no more take the stage tonight and perform the Tchaikovsky at a world-class level with her mind distracted and her emotions running amok than she could play the piece while also juggling a half dozen flaming torches and riding a unicycle.

Julia ruthlessly pushed all thoughts of Slavko into the deepest, darkest corner of her mind and turned out those lights.

Gone.

She cleansed her mind of all emotions apart from those within the Tchaikovsky concerto itself. She immersed herself in the *Allegro moderato*, the *Canzonetta*, and the *Allegro vivacissimo*, and absorbed the crushing emotions of the masterpiece's musical depiction of *Romeo and Juliet* even as the parallels to her own life pierced her heart.

Her art, her career, and her life were on the line.

This was survival mode. And...she...would...survive.

Dressed in the baggiest gray sweatpants and sweatshirt she owned, Julia stood up against the foot of the hotel bed and poured her soul into the music. She made love to the music for hours with the partner she never needed to fear, her violin.

Her dedication and intensity paid off. That evening, her performance was technically flawless and full of the raw energy and fiery emotion that had earned her the title *La Petite Rockette*. The only soul in attendance who could have guessed at the inner agony she'd felt was herself.

Mission accomplished.

Alone backstage in her dressing room, however, the walls of her compartmentalization collapsed, crumbling to dust, and despair crashed over her.

Chapter Twenty-Two

Once again, the silence was deafening. Not from the guys, of course. From Julia. The guys wouldn't shut the hell up.

They started in during a late brunch, several hours after he left Julia, at a greasy spoon diner. The four band members were crammed into one of the twenty booths that ran along the diner's front and side walls. Happy Eddie and Slavko sat on the outside, Silent Wally and Junior inside them, up against a wall with discolored and peeling gray wallpaper. The booth's faded red vinyl upholstery was dotted with blotchy black stains and unsightly tears. A fresh red-and-white checkered paper tablecloth concealed any ills on the tabletop surface beneath it.

The clatter of silverware on plates and the buzz of conversation filled the place. The smells of bacon, sausage, and coffee hung in the air even before their orders arrived and were then joined by the aromas of omelets with peppers and onions, pancakes, and French toast. Happy Eddie had, of course, ordered the Hungry Man's Special and its three plates loaded with food surrounded him.

"So, Romeo, you gonna have the energy for two shows tonight?" Happy Eddie said with a big Santa Claus chuckle before shoveling in a forkful of scrambled eggs.

"Yeah, or are we gonna have to prop you up like that guy in the movie," Junior said from diagonally across the table with an impish grin.

"*Weekend at Bernie's*," Happy Eddie added.

"Yeah, that one," Junior said.

"Don't you clowns worry about me," Slavko said, and grimly sipped his unsweetened coffee.

"After going at it all night last night," Junior said with a chortle, "he might need *something* propped up for round two tonight."

The rest of them howled with laughter. Happy Eddie's normally ruddy cheeks grew an even deeper shade of red.

"Time for the little blue pill," Junior said, snorting at his own humor. "Although he might have used one last night and ignored that warning to see a doctor if the woody lasts more than four hours."

More howls of laughter. Slavko grinned weakly, feeling no humor in his situation at all but feeling forced to play along.

"Had to be at least four hours last night," Junior said, latching on like a dog to its bone. "Happy Eddie, what time did he get in this morning?"

"What are you guys, my mother?" Slavko asked, trying unsuccessfully to keep his tone light. He winced at how much of a rough edge had come across in his voice. He tried again for a much softer approach. "I mean, I can take a joke as good as anyone. Take your best shot. Go for it." Slavko spread out his arms wide. "But geez, you're sounding like high school kids trying out juvenile, locker room humor for the first time."

Junior's face fell. As the youngest member of the group by far, only twenty-one years old, the disparaging reference to high school and juvenile humor had apparently hit too close to home.

"Hey, I didn't mean it that way," Slavko said, trying to repair the damage even though he wasn't sure exactly what way he could have meant it that wouldn't have delivered the same broadside to Junior's ego.

He stabbed a piece of his omelet and shoved it in his mouth. He was sure it tasted fine, at least according to what his taste buds must be telling his brain, but you could have fooled him. The omelet tasted like shit. The hash browns tasted like shit. His coffee tasted like shit.

His life had turned to shit. From Heaven to Hell. All because of one slip of the tongue.

If only Julia would message him that they could at least talk tonight. That he still had a chance. He resisted the almost overwhelming urge to check his phone to make sure he hadn't missed a ping. He knew it was far too early to expect a message—he'd only caught the Uber from the hotel several hours earlier and Julia had made clear she needed to prepare for her concert tonight—and in fact, there was no guarantee she'd message him at all. This morning, this afternoon, this evening.

Or ever.

Her continued silence would be its own death knell of an answer. All because, while half asleep, he'd blurted out Julia's name. He supposed there would have been trouble eventually. There was no avoiding it. He was the world's worst liar. He liked to think it was from an almost total lack of practice, but he had to admit that could be self-delusional nonsense. One way or another, however, a slip had been inevitable. If it hadn't come while half asleep, wouldn't he have eventually spoken it during the heights of passion?

Perhaps it had subconsciously been intentional. His subconscious had wanted—had maybe even *needed*—to expose his lie of omission. *Lies* of omission, plural. That he not only knew Julia's name, he knew all publicly available information about her life. And he had *known* they would fortuitously be in Buffalo the same weekend even while pretending to toss nothing better than dart throws of dates and locations.

A parade of lies of omission. Deception on a grand scale.

So maybe his subconscious had intentionally slipped, had deliberately exposed his deceptions because it wanted total honesty—it *needed* total honesty—with a woman with whom he had somehow decided, quite insanely after a mere handful of nights together, that he wanted to spend the rest of his life. That she was a goddess, and he simply *had* to spend his life with her.

Or perhaps his subconscious simply had a romantic death wish.

"Slavko," Happy Eddie said in a voice that seemed to be coming from far away. "Earth to Slavko."

Slavko blinked. He shook his head, attempting to clear the cobwebs. "What were you saying?"

"I was asking you what's wrong when you zoned out on me," Happy Eddie said. "Don't try to say 'nothing'. I know you too well for that. Something's wrong. I know I gave you crap a couple weeks ago for having a huge smile on your face while the rest of us were dying inside, but I take it back. Now you've gone in the other direction. You got your ashes hauled all last night, but this morning you're miserable. What gives?"

Hoping to deflect the question, Slavko replied, "I wasn't getting my ashes hauled *all* last night. I couldn't have lasted longer than three, three and a half hours."

Junior laughed, but Happy Eddie didn't crack a smile.

"Something's wrong," Happy Eddie said. "I can tell. Are you okay?"

"I'll be fine," Slavko said, though he knew that if Julia never got back to him, he would very much *not* be fine.

"Is it band business?" Happy Eddie asked. "Has something else gone wrong?"

"It isn't band business," Slavko said. "Business sucks. We've got problems. But you all know that. There's nothing about the band that you don't already know. All those cards are on table, face up."

Happy Eddie nodded.

"It's personal." Slavko stared into his coffee. "It's complicated."

Silence fell as if the boys expected him to say more. But Slavko had nothing.

"Okay, then," Happy Eddie said. "None of us wants to pry into your personal affairs. But as you go, so goes the band. We all know that. And right now, Romeo looks like Juliet ran him over with the bus."

The seconds ticked by with no word from Julia. Sixty of those slow-as-molasses seconds became a minute, still with no word from Julia. Sixty minutes became an agonizing hour with no word from Julia.

Finally, it was show time. And the show must go on. Two of them on this night, to be precise. Slavko had to put his big boy pants on and give the customers what they'd paid to see and hear.

And he did. Even when couples took to the dance floor, beaming their love to each other. Big boy pants on. Keep those beaming smiles on those couples' faces. Forget that you may never smile like that again.

Slavko proved once again that there was no better polka tuba player in the world. And when it came to dueling accordion solos, he and Happy Eddie played second fiddle to no one. The Pied Piper Polish Polka Dots delivered a great first show and then topped that two hours later. They even got paid as promised, could he get a hallelujah! But as Slavko wiped off his tuba and placed it in its black hard-shell case, he did so with a sinking heart.

The silence from Julia had gone from deafening to soul-crushing. There had been no ping signifying a message. Not throughout the morning, the afternoon, or the two shows this evening.

It was over. Slavko knew it. He felt hollow and empty inside.

If his subconscious had deliberately ratted him out to Julia, he was no longer on speaking terms with his damned self-righteous subconscious. And if he never got to see Julia ever again, all because of an obsession with honesty that didn't allow for even the most well-intentioned lies of omission, then to hell with honesty.

To hell with everything.

His phone pinged.

Chapter Twenty-Three

They sat together on the king-size bed in Julia's "love nest" hotel room, their backs up against the dark gray upholstered headboard, cushioned by two fluffy pillows. They were fully clothed, having discarded only their shoes, Slavko in a rugged-looking, red-and-white plaid flannel shirt and black jeans that made him look enticingly like the lumberjack Paul Bunyan, Julia in a flowery tan blouse and matching slacks.

She had, of course, abandoned the pretense of a disguise, except for the usual rust-colored wig, baseball cap, and oversized sunglasses on the way over from her official hotel and had ditched all of those as soon as she arrived. No contact lenses to turn her soft brown eyes to bright blue. Just her in her in her most plain state: long black hair tied back, no jewelry other than her watch, and only a few dabs of lavender-scented perfume just in case.

She tried to ignore Slavko's pleasing cedarwood scent and the closeness—just inches away—of that wonderful body of his that had given her so much pleasure. She also tried to ignore that boyishly innocent face with its winsome smile. Most of all, she tried to ignore that big heart of his that had stolen hers away.

Stolen her heart and prompted her to break all her rules. No second dates. No emotion. And certainly none of the L word.

Now look at where that had gotten her. Pushed a career she'd spent her entire life on to the brink of a cliff, staring down at an unknown abyss if her actions were found out and deemed as scandalous as she was sure the stuffed shirts would conclude. Scandalous confirmation about the lies they'd suspected were true all along.

"I was on pins and needles until I got your message," Slavko said.

"I was on pins and needles until I sent it. Still am."

"I wasn't even sure if '*Let's meet tonight, we'll talk*' was good news or bad news."

"To tell the truth, I wasn't sure either. I'm still not sure."

Slavko had expected a little more clarity than that, but he wasn't going to complain. At least the two of them were here. Together.

"I was glad," he said, "you were at least giving me the chance to see you at least one more time and state my case."

"I wanted to see you, too," Julia said. "I just don't know what to do."

Slavko gave a half-hearted chuckle. "I had to hope you hadn't decided the best way to silence your secret was to bring me here and kill me."

"I hadn't thought of that." Julia laughed. "Good idea."

"Guess I shouldn't have brought it up."

"Not a smart move, but I'm glad you did," Julia said. "Know where I can get a gun? Or do you prefer poison?"

"I prefer to die of old age," Slavko said. He drew in a breath as if to say something more, but slowly exhaled and remained silent.

"Let me guess," Julia said. "You wanted to add something, but it would have broken the rules. My rules. About the L word and all that. What you wanted to say was, 'I prefer to die of old age...in the arms of the woman I love.'"

Slavko whirled onto his side to face her. He shook his head. "You're spooky."

"Nah," Julia said softly. "You're just easy to read. You wear your heart on your sleeve."

Silence hung in the air.

"Listen, I don't know what's going to happen here," Julia said. "I'm a mess. My mind is a jumble. My heart is torn in two. But at least for tonight—because who knows if for us there is a tomorrow—let's forget the rules. Speak your mind. Speak from your heart because hearing the unvarnished truth is the only way I'll know what to do."

"Good. Consider me an open book," Slavko said. "I'll tell you anything you want to know. Even the PIN code on my phone." He rested his hand on Julia's thigh. "And you can tell me as much or as little about yourself as you want."

Julia took his hand from her thigh and put it back on his. "I'm not sure that you touching me is a good thing right now. Even something as innocent as a hand on my thigh. When I'm not with you, I long for your touch. And when I am with you, the very touch of your fingertips practically sets my hair on fire."

"Is that what happened to that godawful wig?"

Julia roared with laughter. "It was pretty bad, wasn't it?"

"Like a moustache on the Mona Lisa."

"My point is that we can't get distracted. Not tonight. And you distract the hell out of me."

"I'll take that as a compliment, thank you," Slavko said. "And for what you do to me, the word distract doesn't begin to describe it. So I'll keep my hands to myself."

Julia nodded. "So where do we start? Since a lot of my life story is online, should I assume you've read a lot of it?"

"Well...um..yeah," Slavko admitted. "If I could find it, I read it. You're a fascinating person who has lived—is living—a fascinating life. You're the best in the world at what you do."

"One of the best," Julia corrected.

"But there's nothing about your personal life," Slavko said. "For someone as famous as you are, that's rare. It's as if you have no life outside of your music."

"That's pretty much how it is," Julia said. "It's a cutthroat world. The competition is *insane.* There isn't the time and energy for a personal life. Sarah Chang is the solo violinist I'm most often compared to. Probably because she's Asian and pretty. She's Korean and I'm Chinese, but you know how it is for a lot of white people. All Asians look alike." Julia glanced at Slavko. "No offense."

"None taken."

"Anyway, Sarah Chang was accepted to begin studying at Julliard at the age of five! *Five! At Julliard!* That's incomprehensible! Five years old!" She glanced at Slavko and saw that he was more than suitably astonished. He wasn't sure he believed his ears. She figured she'd better explain. "Julliard is the most prestigious—"

Slavko waved the explanation away. "I know Julliard. That does seem impossible."

"That's my competition!" Julia said, reflexively cranking up the volume to match her emotions. "She debuted for the New York Philharmonic at the age of eight! *Eight!* Performed the Paganini without even a single practice with the orchestra and crushed it anyway! Brought the house down! Recorded her first album at the age of ten.

"I was considered by many a prodigy—I debuted with the Boston Symphony at the age of twelve—but compared to Sarah Chang, I was a late bloomer, a dolt with no talent at all. She was a musical Einstein. I was a musical...*nothing.* With no hope of ever catching up.

"Even today, one of the celebrity websites comments that she's forty-three, isn't married, and 'is known to have been in at least one relation-ship.' That's a direct quote. Forty-three and has been in *one* relationship!" Julia thrust her index finger at Slavko. "*One relationship! Forty-three years old!* Either she's insanely private like I am, or she's every bit as obsessed. Or both."

Julia took a deep breath and realized she'd almost been shouting. But if she was going to shout about anything, this would be it.

"Sorry about laying it on a little thick there," she said, giving Slavko a quick pat on the thigh. "But you have to understand how impossible my competition is and, even worse, the awful things said about me when my career began to take off. The rumors were as vicious as they were untrue. The worst of the scandal-mongering critics and some of my jealous rivals whose careers were stalling insinuated that it was whatever beauty I possessed that fueled my success.

"A mediocre talent with a pretty face. That's all I was. And then when that didn't topple me, the rumors became that I'd slept my way to the top. Got there on my back. Especially after two conductors I'd worked with got nailed for sexual harassment. I'd fended them off, apparently unlike others, but somehow I was deemed guilty. I must have said *yes* to get ahead. Not that I got ahead despite saying *no*.

"Dammit, I took what talent I was blessed with and then outworked *everyone*. *No one* practiced and studied harder than I did! And still do! So maybe you can understand now why I'm just a wee bit sensitive to anything that merely *hints* of scandal. I can't let those bastards nod and say, 'I told you so!'"

Julia exhaled forcefully. She grinned sheepishly. "I did it again, didn't I? Couldn't even let you get a word in edgewise."

"Silenced me as totally as when you sit on my face."

Julia burst out laughing. And as the laughter rolled over her, the crushing weight she'd been feeling lifted. Not entirely, but a lot. Slavko seemed to know how to make her feel better in so many ways.

"Don't get talking about that," she said. "I won't be able to think straight."

"I guess that's two of us," he said with a smile, then took in a deep breath, as if signaling that the frivolity was over.

And it was.

"I'm glad you told me everything," Slavko said. "I'd wrap my arms around you and hold you tight if that weren't against tonight's rules."

"Then break the damned rules."

Several minutes and a multitude of long kisses and caresses later, their clothes were still on, zippers still zipped, and buttons still buttoned, but both looked a bit rumpled. Slavko's arm was looped around Julia's neck. Her head was nestled comfortably against his shoulder.

It felt wonderful.

"I needed that," Julia said, and burrowed her head more deeply against his shoulder. "Thank you."

"I wish I could hold you like that every night."

Julia sighed. "Time for you to talk."

"If I can say only one thing," Slavko said, "it's that yes, I now know who you are and know your allegedly dirty little secret. Which is me. I can appreciate that because of things unfairly said about you in the past, you feel you're vulnerable to that secret being exposed. Theoretically, I could expose you and then you'd find out if that secret is, in fact, as destructive as you fear.

"But there's no cramming the genie back in that bottle. I'm always going to know. There's no changing that, whether you stay with me or leave me. So why not stay with me? I'm crazy about you and I think you're at least a little bit crazy about me."

Julia considered responding that she was, in fact, full-out crazy. Yes, crazy about him. She had to admit that. But also plain old crazy. Batshit crazy. Or if she wasn't there yet, she was on her way and breaking the speed limit. No one would ever call her normal.

Instead, she said, "Back up. You're like a lawyer giving your closing arguments even though the trial is only starting."

"This is a trial?" Slavko asked.

Julia could tell his eyebrows had shot up in surprise without even looking.

"It's a figure of speech," she said. "But it's also true. We're both trying to decide which way to turn in our relationship. Have we hit a dead end or not?"

"Your honor," Slavko said, "my decision is made up. I'm guilty of only one thing and that's loving you. I'm not guilty and never will be guilty of betraying you. Your secret will never leave this courtroom."

Julia laughed despite the gravity of what they were discussing, and she guessed Slavko's humor was solely a defense mechanism to get over the fear of losing her.

"Well, the court," she said, "would like to learn a little bit more about the witness before it can feel completely comfortable in the veracity of his words. No witness comes into this courtroom"—Julia gestured to the hotel room's TV, desk, and chair like a game show hostess—"no one comes in here and says, 'I am an untrustworthy scum of the Earth.'"

"I throw myself at the mercy of the court," Slavko said.

"Slavko, I don't know anything about you," Julia said, deciding to drop the courtroom-lawyer-and-judge bit. "I feel I've looked into your heart and found it's a big one, but I don't even know your last name. How can I feel comfortable knowing an almost total stranger could possibly destroy me?"

"My name is Slavko Novak," he said. "And on my life and that of my family, I would never destroy you. *Could* never destroy you."

"Novak. What nationality is that? My mother would only care that you are not Chinese, but I'm curious."

"Slovakian. My grandparents came to this country from what was then known as Czechoslovakia."

"Slavko the Slovakian. It has a ring to it. I like it." Julia nestled more snugly against his shoulder. "Tell me more about yourself. What's important to you?"

"I'm a musician," Slavko said.

Julia sat bolt upright. She stared at him in astonishment. *"You are? Seriously?"*

Slavko nodded and grinned sheepishly. "See? I can keep a secret."

Julia swatted him playfully. "You sonuvabitch." She shook her head, flabbergasted. "Tell me more! No, wait. Let me guess."

"You'll never guess."

"Of course I will."

"If you don't guess it in ten questions, then you have to love me forever," Slavko said with a smirk.

"This will be fun. But I don't want to see your face because you'll give it away." Julia sank back against Slavko's shoulder and snuggled close. She put a hand to her mouth to stifle a giggle. "I want this to be a challenge."

"Ten questions or you have to love me forever," Slavko teased again.

Julia wondered if he might not teasing after all. She'd been running away from the L word since almost the first night that they'd met. Perhaps, despite all her defenses, it had snuck up and caught her.

She pushed the thought away. *Just have fun, dammit! He's a musician. How exciting!*

"I'm sorry I don't recognize your name," she said, suddenly fearful that he might be reasonably well known and her ignorance could be considered insulting. "I don't follow much popular music. Only a little."

"Is that a question? You only get ten."

"No. Let me think." Julia felt like a little girl trying to guess the answer to a tricky riddle. Narrow it down. She had to narrow it down. Think!

"I'm going to guess that you play an instrument," she said. "You might sing a little, but you're primarily an instrumentalist."

"You're right!" Slavko said, sounding surprised. "How did you guess that?"

"I'm not just a pretty face," Julia said gleefully. She stroked Slavko's barrel of a chest. "I've found out in the most wonderful way that you have exceptional lung capacity and absolutely magical lips when it comes to lovemaking, so that would argue for a brass or woodwind instrument as opposed to strings or percussion. Could be either one. And almost certainly something with a demanding embouchure to give you those magical lips. I'm going to guess woodwinds."

"*Pffft!*" Slavko sounded, mimicking a buzzer. "Wrong. Eight more questions."

"So it's got to be brass," Julia said. "Going by the numbers, the highest probability would be the trumpet."

"*Pffft!*" Slavko sounded again. "Seven more questions."

"Not a trumpet?" Julia was stunned. She thought she'd nailed that one. "It couldn't be trombone, could it?"

"*Pffft!* Six more."

"Hold on. Maybe I'm going in the wrong direction. You could be in a full orchestra, a chamber orchestra, or maybe even a band. Are you in an orchestra of some size?"

"*Pffft!* Five more questions."

"No?" Julia cried. "Now I'm in trouble."

In a playground, singsong voice, Slavko sang, "She's going to love me forever. She's going to love me forever. She's going to love me forever."

"Quiet," Julia giggled. "Let me think!"

Slavko whispered, "Julia's going to love me forever. Julia's going to love me forever."

She swatted him, then kissed his cheek. "So you're in a band. If it isn't classical or jazz, I'm in trouble. Is it classical or jazz?"

"*Pffft!* Four more questions."

"Yikes. Probably pop music or country, but there are too many genres. And only four more questions. I might as well go for the instrument. A brass instrument that isn't a trumpet or trombone. In an orchestra, that would only leave a horn of some sort or a tuba. God knows what other brass instruments there might be in the other genres."

"Julia's going to love me forever," Slavko whispered in singsong. "Julia's going to love me forever."

"A French horn or one of its variations?"

"*Pffft!* Three more."

"No! Unless there's some obscure brass instrument from a genre I don't know," Julia said, "that just leaves the tuba."

"Is that your guess?"

"It has to be."

"Correct! Tuba!" Slavko said. "But you've got to guess the genre and you only have two questions left." Slavko chortled with glee. "Julia's going to love me forever. Julia's going to love me forever."

"Pop music?" Julia guessed, although with classical and jazz eliminated, she really had no idea. Pop music was simply the largest field.

"*Pffft!* One more question," Slavko cried. "Julia's going to love me forever. Julia's going to love me forever."

"You got me, Slavko," Julia said. "I have no idea."

"What's your last question?" he asked. "Julia's going to love me forever. Julia's going to love me forever."

"I don't know!"

"Guess!"

A silly idea popped into her head and she began to laugh uproariously.

"Just don't tell me that it's polka!" she said, laughing so hard at the hilarious thought that she could barely get the words out. "That you're an oompah, oompah tuba player in a polka band!"

Chapter Twenty-Four

Slavko was eating breakfast in the same diner as the day before with the same smells of bacon, sausage, and coffee. The same buzz of conversation and clinks of silverware on plates rang in the air. He was even sitting in the exact same booth with its torn red upholstery and a fresh red-and-white checked paper tablecloth with the same three bandmates.

But everything had changed.

The night before, he'd gone from once again experiencing Heaven on Earth with Julia to the purest Hell. In a mere split second.

Her laughter still rang in his ears. It delivered fresh cuts to his heart, tearing it apart over and over, like a Jack the Ripper of the soul.

Julia the Ripper.

She had torn him apart with the mockery of her laughter. Not intending to cause him pain, but, even worse, inflicting it ten times over with its instinctive derision. It had been bad enough when those ignorant teenagers at the Topsfield Fair, like others of their ilk elsewhere across the country, had ridiculed the band and its music. Slavko could dismiss the actions of those who wouldn't know duple meter or a subdominant chord if it hit them between the eyeballs.

But Julia was one of the most accomplished musicians in the world, revered from New York to Vienna. Her opinion meant something. Actually, it meant everything. And for her, polka was nothing but a laughingstock.

"Just don't tell me that it's polka!" she had said, barely able to get the words out because of her uncontrollable laughter. "That you're an oompah, oompah tuba player in a polka band!"

Hilarious.

Those peals of laughter. Of unintended but instinctive ridicule and derision.

He'd been a fool, of course, to think, once he'd found out who she was, that it could have ended any other way. She was the female equivalent of Itzhak Perlman, a globe-trotting superstar in the stuffy, snooty world of classical music.

Polar opposites with polka. What the hell had he expected?

But before that nuclear laughter exploded, they had kissed so sweetly and held each other tight, as if holding on for dear life. And then as they continued to talk, his arm had been around her and she'd been nestled snugly against his shoulder.

Where she belonged.

One minute they were laughing and giggling their way through her ten questions and he was chanting in rhythmic singsong, "Julia's going to love me forever. Julia's going to love me forever."

Sweet. Perfect. Joyful.

But then a split second later, she destroyed him forever. Like a thick, lush forest of green burned to the ground by a raging, scorched-earth fire, all that was left of his heart was a lifeless mass of cold, black ashes. But unlike a forest that might eventually spring back to life, Slavko knew the barren soil of his heart would never give life to anything ever again.

"You look like you got run over by a truck," Happy Eddie said as he poured what looked like a gallon of syrup over his stack of pancakes. He said nothing more but raised his Santa Claus bushy eyebrows to ask a question without actually asking it.

None of them had said a word when he'd gotten back to the Motel 6 not much more than an hour after he left. The nervous silence had continued this morning when he'd announced that they were checking out immediately. They could forget that previously mentioned possibility of staying an extra day on his dime. They were leaving immediately after tonight's performances. They were getting the hell out of Dodge, so to speak. No questions asked, if you don't mind. And they'd asked none, just nodded and silently packed. Perhaps, Slavko thought, his anger or sense of crushing humiliation had exuded an invisible "don't mess with me" aura. But he'd known that sooner or later he had to address the elephant in the room.

And so he did in the most blunt, forceful language possible. Because he felt blunt, forceful fury.

"As a matter of fact, I did get run over," Slavko said. "The eighteen-wheeler of love crushed me. Had no lights on, so I never saw it coming. Flattened me like a cheap pancake. Left nothing of my beating heart. Then as it backed up to see if I was all right, it ran right over me again. I guess the Universe wanted to make sure the job got done."

Slavko could only vaguely recall extricating his arm from around the still-roaring-with-laughter Julia the Ripper, then leaping from the bed, and grabbing his jacket to leave.

"Slavko?" she'd said, no longer laughing as she stared up at him from the bed. Wide-eyed. Face turned ashen. "Oh my God, Slavko." A hand to her mouth, aghast. "Is that what...did I...oh my God, I never imagined. I am... I am so sorry. I didn't mean it. I never imagined.... I didn't mean anything. I swear it. I am so sorry."

But her laughter spoke louder than any words of apology. She might be truly sorry. In fact, Slavko was sure that she was. Sorry to have hurt him. He could see it in her eyes, suddenly pooling with tears.

Sorry to have *crushed* him, though she could never imagine the impact of her ridicule.

But her uncontrolled laughter had been *honest.* It conveyed how much of a laughingstock she thought polka was. And even worse, not just polka as a whole but that he was *an oompah, oompah tuba player*, the height of knee-slapping hilarity and the absolute depth of musical accomplishment. Even though, as quite probably the single most accomplished polka tubist in the world, he provided a lot more to the Pied Piper Polish Polka Dots than the occasional oompah, oompah. A hell of a lot more.

Julia's laughter could not have been any more honest. It spoke her true thoughts at decibel levels exceeding jet engines during takeoff. As did the part of her attempted retraction that went, "I never imagined." Slavko could believe that all too well, too. Of course, she never imagined the bull's-eye her ridicule had hit. For sure, she couldn't imagine a *real* musician stooping so low as to be an oompah, oompah tuba player in a polka band.

He recalled the rest as if he'd been in a dreamlike state, but a dream turned nightmare. Julia the Ripper trying to block him from leaving the room. Him brushing past her, forcing his way out the door. Having to get away. Racing down the hotel hallway. Julia tugging at his arm, telling him to stop.

But knowing he couldn't stop. He could never see her the same way again. And neither could she see him.

It was over.

Into the elevator. Together. Through the front lobby, past wide-eyed onlookers, and outside. Julia the Ripper begging him to stop. Saying she *loved* him.

Finally using the L word. After it was too late. Because she had tarnished everything that truly mattered to him with her flippant disrespect. Not just tarnished. Poisoned.

Saying words that could not be un-spoken. Words that could not be un-heard. Laughter that could not be retracted. Laughter and ridicule he thought he would hear in his heart, at some level, for the rest of his life.

Life had no rewind button.

Some things were forever.

And so he had run down the street along the cracked and crumbling sidewalks. Away from the hotel. Away from Julia the Ripper as fast as his legs could carry him. Because it was the only way to escape her clutches.

And since he was faster with legs much longer than hers and a lung capacity she had delighted in while squirming on his face and screaming out her pleasure, he got free.

And would never return.

His passion for polka—his life's work!—was like a cockroach in her eyes. She'd stepped on that carapace—knowing instinctively and beyond a shadow of a doubt that it was ugly—and laughed at the resulting crunch. Twisting her foot to be sure it was dead.

There was no going back from that.

No putting the cockroach back together.

Slavko deleted his DiscreetPartnerForYou account while waiting for the Uber driver to arrive.

"Sorry to hear that, man," Happy Eddie said, a forkful of sausage frozen in the air halfway to his mouth.

"Yeah," Junior said as Silent Wally nodded, then both looked uncomfortably down at their plates.

Slavko couldn't remember exactly what he'd said to prompt those words of sympathy and the somber looks, but he had no doubt as to its reference.

"Thanks," he said, and sipped his coffee. "But I'm going to ask you guys this one favor. In fact, I'm going to insist on it. Okay?"

All three nodded without even waiting to hear what it was.

"I don't ever want to hear a reference to that woman again," Slavko said. "Not a question about her. Not a joke. Not a single thing that indicates she ever lived and came into my life. She is out of my life forever. She is dead to me. And that's the way I want it. That's the way I need it.

"She doesn't even have a way to contact me anymore. I'll never see her again, and I never want to see her again. If I can ever forget her, I'll get down on my knees and thank the heavens for that merciful blessing. So God help any one of you if you dare remind me of that woman."

Chapter Twenty-Five

Julia was heartbroken. *What had she done?* A silly, idle joke and...

...and Slavko had been devastated. By a stupid joke. How was she supposed to have known? She never would have imagined it. Never *could* have imagined it.

Polka? Seriously? *Polka?*

And playing the oompah, oompah tuba! A stud like Slavko?

It had to be a gag and just about the most unbelievable gag ever, Julia had thought, sitting propped up on the bed, the pillow behind her, nestled against Slavko's shoulder one instant, laughing uproariously, only to feel him an instant later pulling away from her and leaping off the bed as if he'd suddenly realized she was a carrier of a horrific disease. She'd been convinced it was all an act until, after that first delayed split second, it registered just how horrified and completely crushed he looked.

Destroyed. Lost. Like a little kid who had just watched his puppy executed.

And she'd been the executioner.

She'd been in his arms and everything was perfect, everything was right, from the cedarwood scent of his cologne to the minty taste of his lips. So perfect. So right. They were laughing and giggling and getting to know each other. He'd listened with genuine interest as she'd rambled on and on—for almost certainly way too long—about the snide accusations made about her sleeping her way to the top. Then he'd kissed her in just the right way to let her know that he understood and sympathized and would always be there for her, holding her tight the way he was right then.

She knew then that she could never say goodbye to him. She might even be willing to not only think the L word but say it aloud. She'd gone from not being sure if she should stay with him to being sure she couldn't live without him. Love—there was that crazy L word again—often made no sense, behaving in mysterious ways no one, least of all her, could fathom.

What she knew was that Slavko wasn't the Serpent in her musical Garden of Eden. He might not be Adam to her Eve—the metaphor fell apart when it got stretched that thin—but he wasn't the problem. No matter how anxious it made her to know that *anyone* knew her secret and could scandalize her fragile reputation, she had believed Slavko's words that he would never betray her.

They had a future.

And then, amidst their laughter and clowning around, she'd unwittingly crushed him. He'd shoved her aside and rushed from the room no matter how hard she tried to stop him. Down the hallway, into the elevator, and out through the lobby. Without her disguise. She didn't care. She cared only that she was losing him no matter how hard she begged for him to stop.

No matter that the words slipped out that she *loved* him. Because she did.

And now he was gone. Possibly forever.

What she found on the Internet astonished her. Slavko Novak, *her* Slavko, had been named the most exceptional polka tuba player in the world *five* times! He and his band, the Pied Piper Polish Polka Dots, had earned an additional four nominations. And of course, they were appearing in

Buffalo this weekend and had appeared in the Topsfield Fair two weeks ago, putting him in her proximity for their nights together.

Most exceptional polka tuba player in the world five times! No wonder he had been insulted by her laughter and unintended ridicule. He was the best in the world and she had spit on his accomplishments. Acted as though they were hilarious.

What had she done?

But how could she ever have known? Much as she wanted to beat herself up over it—and she felt *horrible* about how she'd hurt Slavko—she couldn't see how she could have avoided walking off that particular cliff.

Polka? Slavko? On the oompah, oompah tuba? It boggled the mind.

She knew, of course, of polka's influence on classical music —Shostakovich and Stravinsky immediately came to mind—and the many polkas written by revered composers. The Strauss family had composed many polkas in addition to the waltzes they were most famous for. The *Annen Polka*, the *Im Krapfenwald'l*, and the *Bitte schön! Polka*.

She knew all of that history, but this was different. This was current-day beer halls, kielbasa, schnitzel, and sauerkraut. Corny accordions and, good lord, oompah, oompah tubas.

Slavko was the roundest of pegs in that squarest of holes. She couldn't picture it at all.

It had totally blindsided her. But she was beyond sorry. She was aghast at what she'd done to him.

Belatedly, she thought to open the DiscreetPartnerForYou app on her phone. She'd bear her soul to Slavko and apologize abjectly for her unforgiveable blunder. She'd tell him that she loved him. She knew that now. She wouldn't run away from the L word. And after she poured her heart out to him, they would agree to get together after her concert and she would make things right. She had wronged him, but she would make things right. Because she truly did love the man.

Slavko's code-named DiscreetPartnerForYou account was missing.

Julia's jaw dropped. She pressed buttons furiously on her phone. Double-checked his anonymous ID even though she'd long since memorized it and had records of it in her own account's communications.

But nothing could resurrect his account from the electronic ether. Or the cloud. Or whatever it was.

He was gone. He'd either deleted his DiscreetPartnerForYou account or hidden it from her sight. He'd run away from her physically down the streets of Buffalo and then, surely no more than ten or fifteen minutes after her unintentionally mocking laughter, had severed all virtual contact.

Slavko hated her.

Julia could not blame him. She hated herself.

Her performance, as was typical for most Sundays, was a matinee at three in the afternoon, unlike the 7:00 p.m. starts on Fridays and Saturdays. Based on the schedule posted on the Pied Piper Polish Polka Dots website, she would have time to rush over to the Wings & Kielbasa Bar for their evening performance and beg forgiveness from Slavko.

If only...

If only she weren't also committed to a fundraising gala for the Philharmonic after the concert. Contractually committed. Her appearance to hobknob with donors was supposedly a key attraction, so it was written into the contract with significant financial penalties assessed if for any reason she failed to appear. She desperately wanted to beg off and right now couldn't care less about the money—*keep it all, dammit!*—but Julia took her contracts seriously and knew that those who didn't feed the monster of the donor factory were committing career suicide.

Besides, was sure she could get to the Wings & Kielbasa Bar in time. The band might be packing up, but she wouldn't miss out on Slavko. And just in case, she would email Slavko using the contact information on the band's website.

Julia missed out on Slavko.

It had been impossible to extricate herself from the fundraising gala early. She'd been assigned presentations and scripted comments throughout the agenda all the way to a closing thank you. The maddening frustration had grown and grown within her as the gala dragged on and on until finally, mercifully, it came to a close.

She rushed into an empty Wings & Kielbasa Bar, empty except for a bald-headed, tall bartender cashing out and a short, stocky member of the custodial staff sweeping the floor.

"No!" Julia cried out, unbuttoning her long, navy blue coat. To both of them, she asked, "Where's the band? I have to talk to one of them. It's important."

"They left about fifteen minutes ago," the bartender said with a shrug and a sympathetic smile. "And that was after two encores. Put on quite a show. Made a lot of people happy."

Chapter Twenty-Six

Another weekend, another Motel 6. Two guys in the beds and two on the floor. And before the weekend, more midweek nights sleeping in the Explorer, thinking fondly of the luxury of a Motel 6. Beds. Heat. Hot showers. Hell, Slavko thought, pretty soon they'd need to get the damned Explorer fumigated. As long as that service was free. And of course, they were feasting once again on Costco free samples.

Life in the polka fast lane. *One and two, three and four. One and two, three and four.*

Julia the Ripper had been right to laugh at what his dream had become. Who could blame her? This life was a joke.

He was a joke.

Slavko wanted to slap his knee at that hilarity. He wanted to slap his face at his monumental stupidity. And he wanted to slap his career to see if he could rouse it from its coma.

Wake the hell up! he want to shout and deliver an extra hard slap.

Slavko was physically awake, taking his turn behind the wheel of the Explorer, even if his career was as dead as his emotions. Unable to sleep, he was driving through the darkness on I-390, wanting to get as far from Buffalo as fast as possible. Heat blasted from the front panel vents. An indie pop station played on the front radio speakers so softly it was barely audible. Slavko didn't want to disrupt the sleep of his bandmates. He just needed something to hide the silence. He'd chosen this station to get a break from Happy Eddie's constant choice of country. Jazz was nowhere to be found on the radio dial, and Slavko sure as hell wasn't going with classical.

They were headed to a weekend gig in Middletown, more than three hundred miles toward New York City. The Helluva Horrific Howling Halloween Hocus-Pocus-Polka Dance Weekend was a mainstay of the band's tour every year. Always a highlight. Slavko built each year's fall schedule around two things, Oktoberfest and this weekend. If anything was going to revive his spirits, this would be it, especially coming on the heels of that night's strong performance by the band and the enthusiastic audience response even with him operating on autopilot. Couples had danced the polka during almost every number.

A great night. Just what the band needed.

Yet Slavko still felt dead inside. His impromptu comment to the boys over breakfast that he'd been run over by the eighteen-wheeler of love hadn't just been flowery language, cringeworthy now some sixteen or seventeen hours later. No, it was how he felt.

Lovers could sometimes say hurtful things they didn't really mean. He didn't have much experience at love, but he thought those hurtful things deserved forgiveness. Relationships that lasted only as long as the first cutting phrase weren't going to survive very long.

This was different. Nothing could heal the fatal cuts from Julia's sharp knife slicing through his mind. There was no changing the death knell it had delivered to what he and Julia had shared. He had bled out. There was no reviving him.

Julia hadn't meant to hurt him. And he could even forgive that hurt.

But her uproarious laughter conveyed with an absolute certainty that she viewed polka as the ultimate musical laughingstock. And if it were possible to slide even lower than that, playing polka music on an oompah, oompah tuba would be it.

She believed in her heart of hearts that his life's work was worthless.

Worthy only of ridicule and derision, not respect. Scorn and contempt, not approval. She was free to have that opinion, of course, and perhaps she was even right. Plenty of people shared it. The Grammy Awards sure did. But following this dream was soul-crushingly hard enough—from getting stiffed by bar owners to the ridicule of ignorant strangers to sleeping in your vehicle at night to scrounging free samples at Costco—without having the person closest to you, the person you love with all your heart, feel contempt for those hopes and dreams, *even if she could remain silent about it.*

Julia could stifle the laughter and maybe even pretend to be impressed, but she would still look at him and secretly see only...a fool. Perhaps a loveable fool. And one whose silly musical passion even made him world class at giving oral sex.

But he would forever be a fool in her eyes.

He probably was. His high school band director had encouraged Slavko to pursue classical music, not polka. Slavko had the chops. The director promised to nominate him to perform the Vaughan Williams Tuba Concerto with the regional orchestra in their district and see how far that experience could take Slavko. Yes, he was that technically proficient. He should do it, the director had argued. Slavko owed it to himself to strive for the sense of profound accomplishment that only classical music and its rigors could give.

But Slavko loved polka. It was in his blood and heart and soul. You didn't follow where prestige and the greatest technical demands might lead you. You followed your heart.

Even if Norma Mae couldn't understand his dream of performing it across the country and maybe eventually, across the world. Even if his mother so often asked when he was going to come home for good and settle down to a real job like working the family farm. And even if Julia the Ripper loved him but considered his art to be a laughingstock.

He still loved Julia. And of course, he would never betray her secret. He would take it to his grave. He simply couldn't remain in a relationship with her, couldn't even be around her, and still survive.

It would destroy his art. It would destroy him.

So when Slavko pulled into a rest stop, prepared to call it a night, and saw Julia's email, his heart sank. He'd pulled into a remote corner of the lot, turned off the ignition, and tilted his seat back ever so slightly. Done for the night, or so he thought.

Her email had come into the band's account. Slavko unavoidably saw the subject line in all capitals: I AM SORRY! I LOVE YOU!

Sadly, he knew he could do only one thing to save himself. It would tear his heart to shreds, but this was a matter of survival.

Without reading a single word of the email, he hit delete.

Chapter Twenty-Seven

Three Weeks Later

Julia sipped her coffee and set it on the small, circular, glass-surfaced table with a soft click. She sat in one of two cushioned chairs beside the table, positioned to face the ten-foot-high by fifteen-foot-wide picture window overlooking the city of San Francisco. A lighted glass chandelier hung overhead. A mahogany dressing cabinet with a full-length mirror facing outward was up against the wall, the king-size bed to its left and the picture window to its right.

The room smelled of fresh flowers arrayed in a vase on the desk fifteen feet away. The pleasing scent would usually have put a smile on her face, or at least provided a subconscious warmth to the ambience, as would have the rich aroma of the coffee.

But nothing was pleasing Julia today or any other day of her almost weeklong stay, even though San Francisco was usually one of her favorite cities. She loved its cable cars, art galleries, museums, and restaurants even though she rarely had time to take advantage of any of them. The last visit, she'd squeezed in only the Asian Art Theatre, a stone's throw from the Davies Symphony Hall where she performed. This visit, she'd squeezed in nothing even though this Sunday matinee would be her final performance.

Dressed in her ugly gray sweatshirt and sweatpants, she sipped again on the coffee and tried to fight off her feeling of helplessness. Had one moment of abject stupidity and insensitivity sentenced her to a life without Slavko? The peculiarities of love befuddled her. She'd kicked the man out of her bedroom not once but twice, only to now feel absolute terror at the thought of never getting him back. And not because she was some shallow manipulator who only wanted something after it had been taken away.

No, she *needed* Slavko. She felt hollow and empty without him. And even though she had a lifetime ago sworn off any emotional attachment with a man, she *loved* Slavko. She felt as if she would die without him.

What's more, she *respected* him and his art. And wasn't her failing to do so—by pouring buckets of freezing cold humiliation on him with her laughter—what had crushed him and sent him running for cover? She could see that now. She'd been wrong not just in the laughter itself but even more cruelly in her fundamental lack of appreciation and respect for his music.

All of that was different now. She didn't merely appreciate that he had achieved awards and great renown in his genre, a genre she'd previously dismissed as laughable and almost pathetic. It wasn't just that in past generations Slavko's music had exerted undeniable influence on the music she loved. It was more than that. It was that Slavko's music in the here and now deserved a respect all of its own.

She'd been studying polka in the weeks since the blowup. Initially, she'd simply wanted to understand Slavko better and appreciate his accomplishments all the more. But the deeper she dove into the genre, the more her respect grew and the more humiliated she felt by her past prejudice. She just needed a way to communicate that to Slavko now, to let him know that she'd been so very, very wrong and she had changed, could he ever forgive her?

Slavko, however, had severed all forms of communication. He clearly wanted nothing to do with her. Unintentionally and in one brief instant, she had become as toxic with her attitude toward his art as her old conservatory friends had been toward hers. She'd been forced to cut the old friends off to save herself. Slavko clearly had done the same. He'd deleted his DiscreetPartnerForYou account and since then had been ignoring her daily, then twice-a-day, and finally three-times-a-day emails to the band's account listed on its website. None of them bounced. He just ignored them, perhaps even putting her account in an auto-delete filter.

There had also been no opportunity to see him in person. She only knew his location for the band's performances and all of them came on the exact same Fridays, Saturdays, and Sundays of her own concerts. As the Pied Piper Polish Polka Dots traversed more of New York state and then Pennsylvania, she performed on those exact same dates multiple time zones away at the Abravanel Hall in Salt Lake City, the Walt Disney Concert Hall in Los Angeles, and now at the Davies Symphony Hall here in San Francisco. The collisions continued well into the future except for the upcoming Thanksgiving week, which she had off but Slavko and the Polka Dots did not.

That left only one option. A roll of love's dice. It was an outrageous gamble, a long shot that might backfire and only make things worse, most likely sealing her fate forever. But she had to do something, and do something more than just talk. It wouldn't be enough to simply *tell* Slavko of her change of attitude and respect. Not even in person. She had to *show* him.

But what a gamble. If it didn't miraculously pay off, she might never laugh and love again. Her inadvertently cruel laughter and its underlying message of what amounted to outright contempt for Slavko's art would serve, romantically speaking, as her own requiem.

She caught the 11:59 p.m. Sunday night red-eye from San Francisco into Pittsburgh, sitting uncomfortably in a middle coach seat since this was the heavily trafficked week of Thanksgiving and she'd booked the flight only days before. A heavy-set, gray-haired businessman in a dark suit sat in the window seat to her left and elbowed her seemingly every time he moved. In the aisle seat to her right, a young Black man wearing a dark green University of San Francisco sweatshirt snored. Julia slept barely a wink before the flight touched down at 9:30 a.m.

Despite her frayed nerves, Julia dutifully called her mother at their appointed time slot, holding off on picking up her car rental so she could call on time. The usual airport public address announcements came over the loudspeakers. Off to the right in baggage claim, blaring alarms sounded that luggage was about to drop down the chute onto the circular rotating belts below.

"You're already at the airport? What time is your flight?" her mother asked, sounding surprised.

"I had a change of plans," Julia explained. "I've actually already landed."

"Already landed? But you hate red-eyes. You swore years ago you'd never take another one."

"Well, something came up," Julia said, not wanting to get into it.

"You're already here in Boston? Will we see you early or not until Thanksgiving Day? It would be great to see you early. Your old bedroom is always available."

"Actually..." Julia took a deep breath and closed her eyes. "I'm not going to be able to make it this year."

The silence of being told you were a horrible daughter thudded on top of her.

"Like I said, something has come up," Julia said feebly.

"Well," her mother said. "That's a sad surprise."

"I'm sorry. This is something I have to do. It's unavoidable."

"Something unavoidable on Thanksgiving Day? What on Earth could be unavoidable on Thanksgiving Day?"

"I'm sorry. When's the last time I wasn't there?"

"You're not even going to explain why?" her mother said.

Julia said nothing because saying what she was thinking would only make things worse.

After a silence that seemed to last forever, her mother said, "We hardly ever see you. Your father will be so disappointed."

"Mother, I'm sorry. I really am. But it can't be helped."

Again, her mother lobbed a silence hand grenade.

"Well," Mother finally said, "I sure hope this unavoidable thing involves a nice young man."

Julia said nothing, but couldn't contain her first smile in a long time.

The owner of the Oktoberfest-All-Year-Round bar opened his office door and let Julia in. He had the look of a grizzled old cowboy, complete with a black ten-gallon hat, white hair, a white beard that extended halfway down his scrawny chest, and a bolo tie. He wore faded jeans and dark brown boots. Only his granny-framed eyeglasses and a black-and-gold Pittsburgh Steelers sweatshirt contradicted the image.

His office walls were festooned with Steelers pennants and framed, signed photographs of players and coaches Julia assumed were former stars. She didn't know football, or hardly any other sports for that matter, from a hole in the wall, but it wasn't hard to put two and two together.

"Name's Tomasz Bratkowski, but everyone just calls me Brat," he said, shaking her hand. "Whaddya want?"

Julia was tempted to try a "Go Steelers" opening line but was pretty sure the guy would see right through her and promptly toss her out. So she got right to the point as he sat down behind a wide desk stacked with piles of paper over almost every inch.

"I have an important favor to ask," she said.

"I don't do favors," he said, and picked up a cigar out of an ashtray and puffed on it even though it wasn't lit. "Nothing in this world is free. Least of all, my time."

"It's about your special show on Thursday night, on Thanksgiving Day."

"We got a great band coming, the Pied Piper Polish Polka Dots,"

Bratkowski said proudly. "And we'll be serving a traditional Polish meal that just begins with a slab of kielbasa on every plate. But it's already sold out, honey, so you're out of luck. I coulda charged an extra five bucks a plate, but that ain't my way. It's a special night for this community." He chomped on his cigar, then grinned. "Only thing coulda ruined it woulda been if the Steelers had one of the games that day. I'da shut down the place in that case."

"I'm sure it will be wonderful," Julia said, "but I'm not looking for extra tickets. What I am looking for"—she swallowed hard—"is that I'm an old friend of a member of that band. It would make what I'm sure will already be a very special night into an even more special night for both him and me." *I sure hope so,* Julia thought. "I'd like to surprise him. On stage. He'll love it!" *And if he doesn't, you'll both want to kill me.* "The audience will love it, too! I promise!" *And sure hope this doesn't blow up in my face.*

"Forget it."

"I flew in all the way from San Francisco," she said.

"You shoulda called."

"I'll make it worth your while," Julia said, and before the old man got any nasty ideas—she'd battled off far too many perverts over the years— she added, "A hundred dollars." She pulled five crisp twenties out of her jeans pocket and fanned them out. "All you'd have to do is let me hide somewhere, maybe even here in this office until they take the stage. Or somewhere else. The band just can't see me until they start playing or the surprise is ruined."

Bratkowski narrowed his eyes. "How can I know you don't bear some sort of grudge against this band and you're just doing this to cause trouble?"

"I swear my intentions are honorable. I swear it on everything I hold dearly. I swear it on all the music you and I both love." She paused, seeing that her reference to music had hit home. Just in case, she added, "Look at me. I'm five feet tall and barely a hundred pounds. I'm no security risk. If you've got a bouncer and I'm doing this to cause trouble—which I swear on my soul I'm not—he'll be able to *dribble* me out the door, I'm so helpless. I'm not here to cause trouble. I have only the sweetest of intentions. I swear it."

Bratkowski grimaced. "I've always had trouble saying no to a woman asking a favor. It just isn't in my makeup. But I'm going to have to. The risk ain't worth a hundred."

"I'll give you two hundred," Julia said. "Make it three. A hundred tonight and two hundred more that night after the band takes the stage, just as long as you've kept it a secret. If my friend knows I'm coming—and I'll know it if he knows—then I don't owe you the extra two hundred. But this will be the easiest three hundred dollars you've ever made." She smiled and needed no mirror to know that a hard-to-turn-down, pleading look was in her eyes. "And you'll also make me very, very happy."

Bratkowski gave a sour smile. "Gimme the hundred."

Chapter Twenty-Eight

Slavko took the steps up onto the thirty-foot-wide stage of the Oktoberfest-All-Year-Round Bar with Happy Eddie, Junior, and Silent Wally in his wake. They all wore the band's trademark red-and-white plaid flannel shirts with black dress jeans. On the wall at the back of the stage, a matching backdrop bore the band's name.

The smells of kielbasa, sauerkraut, and beer filled the air. A bar with a dozen stools, all taken, stretched along the right wall. Every occupant of those stools had turned around to face the stage. An expansive dance floor ran along the left wall, opposite the bar, with eight rows of five tables, all filled, between them.

The buzz of conversation gave way to silent anticipation. Smiling faces looked up at the stage expectantly. Slavko looked out on the packed house of what he estimated to be about two hundred people, all of whom had purchased tickets that included the meal and the show.

He knew on this Thanksgiving Day he should be thankful for this great venue, these appreciative fans, and his three great bandmates, who'd been sticking with him these last three tortured weeks. But his authentic-looking smile to the crowd was forced and frozen and his heart felt like a bleak, arctic landscape where the only thing that was alive was a ravenous polar bear looking for a meal to devour. And that meal was him.

Holidays were the worst time to be alone, and despite the friendship of his three bandmates, Slavko felt unbearably alone. The guys had been great with his cranky moodiness and had lived up to his request that they never once bring up Julia the Ripper, although he had overheard one conversation where she—whose identity was and always would be unknown to them—was referred to as She Who Must Not Be Named. That had actually sent a smile onto his face for a few fleeting nanoseconds, but no warmth had reached his frozen heart.

He couldn't forget Julia no matter how hard he tried. Images of her beautiful face, her long black hair, and her sparkling eyes filled his mind every day. Her laughter haunted all his nights.

He'd have to snap out of it somehow. He knew that. He couldn't go on like this forever. But that eighteen-wheeler of love had pancaked him so firmly to life's asphalt that there was no telling where Slavko Novak ended and the asphalt began.

Well, suck it up, big boy, he told himself as hefted his tuba from its case on the shelf at the back of the stage, clipped in his shoulder strap, and stepped to the microphone. *Give these people what they deserve.* He checked that the others were ready: Happy Eddie on the accordion, Silent Wally on the clarinet, and Junior on trumpet. All systems were go.

"It's great to see all of you here tonight on this wonderful Thanksgiving evening," Slavko said. "Give yourself a hand!"

He waited and the audience gave itself the requested perfunctory applause.

"We hope to give you a great time tonight," he said. "I hope you all have wolfed down your kielbasa and swilled your beer." He stopped theatrically for his oft-repeated line. "I mean, your first *three* kielbasa and your first *six* beers."

The audience laughed warmly, as he'd expected. In times before this barren, arctic spell, he'd drawn energy from that laughter and in no time the band and the audience had formed a symbiotic link, feeding joy and delight back and forth to each other.

But tonight, there was no mutually beneficial symbiosis. He didn't even make a good parasite. He tried to draw on their warmth but felt nothing. As parasites went, he was a dead one.

Well, pull your big boy pants on and deliver, he told himself again, and then added what had lately become a catchphrase that he hoped might eventually become reality.

Fake it till you make it.

"We hope you'll help that kielbasa and beer digest by moving out onto this wonderful dance floor," Slavko said, gesturing to his left. "There's plenty of room for dancing here at the Oktoberfest-All-Year-Round Bar, one of the greatest venues in all the world. So join in whether you're a polka expert or a compete novice who has to speak aloud the words 'one and two, three and four, one and two, three and four.'"

More warm laughter. He guessed almost all of this crowd considered themselves experts.

"We're going to open our show with a number I hope you'll like called "Rock and Rye Polka," Slavko said, and signaled the band's attention with a wave of his index finger. He brought his finger down and they were off.

But...

What was that?

Slavko thought he might be going crazy. Music was emanating from the manager's office, its wooden door wide open, located at the near end of the dance floor.

And not just any music. "Rock and Rye Polka," the exact same song the band was playing. A fiddle was playing "Rock and Rye Polka," and perfectly in sync with the four of them. Playing right along.

What the hell? Who was in that room? And how could they be in sync with the band's every note?

Definitely off my rocker, Slavko thought. But he looked over to Happy Eddie on his left and by the looks of it, Happy Eddie was off his rocker, too. Professional that he was, Happy Eddie was still providing the foundation on his accordion, but his eyes were wide with astonishment and bewilderment. A quick glance to Junior and Silent Wally on Slavko's right confirmed the same.

What the hell?

And then she stepped through the manager's office door.

The bow to her fiddle flew across the strings. Her long black hair was tied back. She was dressed in the band's trademark apparel of a red-and-white plaid flannel shirt and black jeans.

A fearful smile hung on her lips.

Julia!

Slavko's heart skipped one beat and then a second.

Julia!

Slavko kept playing only by stint of having practiced and played every piece in the band's repertoire so many times that every note was etched into his muscle memory. He couldn't forget a note if he tried.

Julia!

What the hell!

Julia!

He couldn't take his eyes off her, even as he sensed the confused looks directed his way from his bandmates.

Julia!

Step by cautious step, she approached the stage, eyes fearful but hands steady on the fiddle's neck and bow. Or was it the *violin's* neck and bow? Julia played the violin, not the fiddle. Then again, he knew they were the exact same instrument, just played differently. If played in a classical music context, it was a violin. If played in this context, it was a fiddle. So Julia was playing the fiddle.

Julia! Playing the fiddle! Here!

Slavko felt as though his mind had been stuffed in a blender and pureed into a thick gray blob.

Julia!

What was she doing here? This was his gig, the band's gig. Was she trying to show off? Muscle into the tiny corner of music he lovingly called his own? Was she trying to take that away, too?

It didn't feel that way at all, but what the hell was she doing here?

She stopped at the stairs to the stage and blinked rapidly, her bow still flying across the fiddle's strings. Slavko could see she was blinking back tears. Blinking faster and faster. But not fast enough. A tear trickled down her beautiful face.

And then without her fiddle and bow missing a beat, she silently mouthed words to him, punctuated by a visible longing in her tear-filled eyes.

I'm sorry!

I was wrong!

You are awesome!

Your music is awesome!

Please forgive me!

Slavko also got the message from the music that flowed out of her fiddle, music that fulfilled the dictum that actions spoke louder than words. Her silently mouthed words apologized and asked forgiveness and said that he and this music was awesome.

But her actions with the fiddle spoke even louder. She was here playing the music to which he had devoted his life. She had learned at least this first tune in their repertoire, probably from one of their records, but hadn't just robotically spewed it out. She had invested the hours needed to understand the polka-specific nuances and imbue her playing with the requisite subtleties.

And in just...what...three weeks?

Perhaps it hadn't been as difficult as he imagined. She was, of course, one of the world's top violin soloists. Even a polka partisan such as himself knew from his days back in high school when he straddled the two worlds that the technical demands of an elite classical music violinist topped those of his counterpart in the polka world. Nowhere near as much a difference as the snooty high brows assumed when they denigrated his genre, but there was no denying the difference.

Even so, Julia had cared enough to do all of that.

And she was here showing him with her loud-as-hell actions that she was sorry and she understood and yes, she loved and respected him.

Julia! Julia! Julia!

When the song ended, Slavko motioned her up the stairs onto the stage.

"We have a surprise guest for you tonight!" Slavko announced after the long and hearty applause died down. "A surprise even for the band. A wonderful surprise!"

Slavko stopped, suddenly stymied by Julia's need for privacy. What could he say now that wouldn't violate that need?

"Our surprise guest on the fiddle is...well...she's our mystery guest. Let's just say she's an old friend and leave it at that," he said.

Julia beamed, her soft brown eyes sparking. She stepped to Slavko's microphone, holding the neck and bow of the fiddle in her left hand, then used the other to point the mic downward to adjust for her shorter height.

Slavko held his breath, not sure what was coming. Had even those benign words of his been too much? Had all his best intentions still set her off and possibly ruined everything?

"Might as well get this out in the open," she said, smiling brightly to the crowd. "No secrets after tonight. My name is Julia Chu. I usually play classical violin, so thank you to Slavko and the boys and especially Mr. Bratkowski, the owner of this wonderful establishment, for indulging me this amazing opportunity." She started to back away, but then stopped. "May I be allowed one more indulgence?" Her eyes lit up. "I *love* this man!"

She turned to Slavko and to his amazement, gently guided the tuba away from his chest and off to the side, cradled the back of his neck, and pulled him close.

She kissed him long and hard. Wonderfully long and wonderfully hard. As if Valentine's Day lasted all year.

The greatest kiss of his life.

Whistles and applause sounded from the crowd.

When the amazing kiss finally ended, Julia said to the crowd, "More than just friends," and flashed a blindingly brilliant smile.

The audience howled with laughter, then clapped, whistled, and hooted with delight some more.

Softly to Slavko, she whispered, "I'm fading into the background now. This is your show." And then as she moved to the back of the stage, she said, "Just know that I love you."

Slavko nodded, his stunned brain still trying to take it all in.

They continued with the next three songs in their planned set list and true to her word, Julia remained in the background even while playing flawlessly. The dance floor filled up each time with delighted couples having the time of their lives.

Inspiration struck Slavko as the applause died down from that third song. He whispered first to Julia, who beamed and nodded her approval, then huddled quickly with the rest of the band. Their eyes widened, but each of them gave a somewhat frightened assent.

"You know, folks," Slavko said, "we have a unique opportunity here. The Pied Piper Polish Polka Dots don't usually have a fiddle player, much less a virtuoso who tours the world as *the* preeminent violin soloist playing with world-renowned orchestras from New York to Vienna. So what do you folks think about us playing a polka tune we've never recorded or played in public before so we can showcase our guest fiddle virtuoso?"

The crowd roared its approval, including several loud whistles.

"Okay, then," Slavko said. "This will be the musical equivalent of a high wire act without a net, but for the first time ever, I give you the Pied Piper Polish Polka Dots with special guest Julia Chu playing 'Cajun Fiddle Polka.'"

And off they went with it. Julia was predictably magnificent. Happy Eddie and Junior looked like they couldn't decide whether to be delighted at the challenge or shit their pants. Silent Wally, as usual, said nothing and just played on.

With the experiment a roaring success and not even a hint of jealousy or resentment toward Julia on the part of the boys, Slavko mixed more of the band's standards with unfamiliar pieces starring Julia like "Fiddling Around Polka," then later, "Fiddle-De-Dee Polka," followed by its musical cousin, "Fiddle-De-Dum Polka."

The crowd *adored* the band and Julia even more, calling for three encores and might have tried for a fourth if Slavko hadn't closed out the third one with the words, "We love you all to death, but this has to be absolutely, positively, unequivocally our final song of the night. Thank you all!"

And when the final note was sounded and the audience roared its appreciation, the band joined hands, Slavko taking Julia's on the right and Happy Eddie's on the left, raised them high, and bowed in splendid satisfaction.

Heaven had come to Earth.

Epilogue

Six Months Later

Julia and Slavko sat on a wooden park bench, hand in hand, there in Vienna, Austria, the City of Music. They looked out over the lush expanse of the park's thick green lawn, which was interspersed with maple trees every couple hundred feet. The smell was clean and fresh. The lightest of breezes fluttered over them and the handful of other couples off in the distance enjoying the late May sunshine and the pristine view.

She and Slavko had walked languidly from the *Museum der Johann Strauss Dynastie*, his arm around her shoulder and hers around his waist. They'd spent several fascinating hours in the recently reopened museum. While the Strauss family of composers was best remembered for their waltzes, most notably the younger Strauss's iconic "The Blue Danube," Julia made sure they lingered at the exhibits relevant to the family's polka compositions which had also stood the test of time.

She loved the city. Musical giants from Beethoven to Mozart had called it home, and it still pulsed to the beat of that music. But she also had to be considerate and recognize that its abundance of riches for her own interests dwindled to far more sparse ones for Slavko. It was why she had suggested the Strauss museum.

"I have a surprise for you," Julia said, and lifted her head off Slavko's shoulder where it had been resting peacefully while she'd waited for the right time. She turned to face him.

"Oh, really?" Slavko said with a mischievous twinkle in his eye. "You have a gift for surprises, but it'll be tough to top that shocker of yours six months ago and all the ones since."

Julia beamed. She'd been scared to death that night as she stepped out of the bar manager's office playing her "fiddle"—not the Stradivarius but one of her other violins and bows better suited for polka's demands and the bar's acoustics—scared to death that Slavko would reject her. Scared to death that she'd hurt him so badly the damage was irreparable. Scared to death that they were finished and nothing she could do would change that. But she'd had nothing to lose with her gamble as stepped out of the bar manager's office that night—it had been impossible to make things worse—and everything to gain.

And wow, had the gamble paid off.

They'd followed that Thanksgiving Day event with additional performances the next three nights. In response, a local newspaper ran a feature story on the oddity of a world-renowned violin virtuoso playing polka music, of all things, in a local bar. The Associated Press picked up on it, expanded the story, and released it, dubbing her and Slavko, "The Odd Couple." The title would be repeated *ad infinitum* and *ad nauseam*, especially after the AP story spawned imitators on the Internet that promptly went viral.

Everyone in Julia's world, from her manager to her record company representative and seemingly everyone in between, was horrified at her "slumming" in the polka world—"destroying her brand," according to a marketing executive—and claimed she would forever damage her reputation if she ever "pulled that stunt" again.

They changed their opinion when Julia and Slavko began making appearances together on the TV late night talk shows as the latest viral sensation. Record sales and requests for performance dates skyrocketed both for Julia and the Pied Piper Polish Polka Dots. When she and Slavko eventually earned placement on the cover of *Rolling Stone*, the magazine couldn't help trotting the "Odd Couple" title out yet one more time. Slavko suggested wryly they might even need to revise their birth certificates.

The stuffed shirts at many of Julia's concerts, not to mention, of course, her mother, could not hide their disdain for Slavko and the Pied Piper Polish Polka Dots. *Whatever had she been thinking?* was the thought either verbalized—in her mother's case with a *tidal wave* of verbalizing— or couched in transparent euphemisms and frozen, backstabbing smiles.

But Julia figured she was a big girl, albeit a petite one, still *La Petite Rockette*, and she could roll with the punches. Even from her mother.

Soon, a European tour was formed for the Pied Piper Polish Polka Dots to the delight of all five of them. Sometimes they performed as the quartet they'd always been, and other times, when it could be wedged into her own tour schedule, with Julia on fiddle. One garishly colored concert poster in France even portrayed Julia and Slavko hilariously as heavy- weight boxers vying for a title with the words *La Petite Rockette vs. Le Grand Tubiste.*

Either way, quartet or quintet, the members of the band, suddenly world travelers, couldn't be happier. Their cramped, chilly nights of sleeping in the Ford Explorer were over. Their days of wandering through a Costco, shoveling in whatever free samples they could scrounge up, were over. Silent Wally even announced, "This is great!"

All of which had led them here to Vienna, Julia's favorite city in all of Europe, if not the entire world, for a week of concerts. And so it was here that she would announce her surprise to Slavko.

"If you don't like the idea, just say so," she said. "This is one hundred percent your call. I won't be offended at all if you don't like it. Just say so."

In truth, Julia knew it would be hard and actually impossible not to be disappointed. This was such a great opportunity and such an exhila- rating challenge. She could barely contain her excitement. But she wouldn't force it on Slavko, wouldn't exert even the slightest pressure.

"What is it?" he asked. "You've piqued my curiosity."

"You've talked about how you played classical music in high school," Julia said tentatively, checking to see if Slavko would give any hints to his reaction but coming up empty. "But I know polka will always be your first love."

"You, my darling, are my first love now," he replied with a boyish grin which, combined with his words, Julia found seductive as all hell. But there would be time enough for that later. Lots of time.

"You know what I mean." She laughed and squeezed his hand. "And you're my first love, too."

They shared so much warm laughter, Julia sometimes thought life couldn't be any better. But perhaps they might squeeze just a tiny bit more joy out of it.

"As I was saying, I know polka will always be your first love, at least your first *musical* love," she said, struggling to control the excitement bubbling up inside her. "But I know an amazing composer who has created some of the best new pieces in the classical music repertory. So I made an initial inquiry. No promises. No commitment on my part. Just an inquiry."

"Spit it out," Slavko said.

"I asked her about a new project I thought of, and she's fascinated by it, actually interested to the point of being eager to start," Julia said. "It'll be new and different, which is always fun and exciting but sometimes terrifying too."

Slavko leaned closer. "You are such a tease. Tell me what it is!"

"I'd like to commission her to write a concerto for the most unusual combination in the repertoire. It's hardly ever been done and only on the margins. Certainly not this way. I want her to write a concerto for tuba and violin! For us!"

Slavko's jaw dropped. "You're kidding!"

"No! What do you think?"

"That's amazing!" he said. "I'd have to go back and brush up on certain techniques I haven't used for several years, but that would be so much fun! So exciting!"

"You like it?"

"I love it!" he said with boyish glee as they hugged, pulled back to look at each other, then hugged again. "What a brilliant idea! And this would be...for us?'

"As far as I'm concerned, there's no other tuba player in the world."

"I bet you say that to all the boys!"

"You, my love, and only you!" Julia said with a laugh. "If it comes out the way I hope, we'll get a record deal set up for it, and you and I will introduce the piece to the entire musical world in a grand premiere. We'll hold a performance exclusive until a bit after the record releases."

"They'll call it the Odd Couple Concerto!" Slavko said, and together they dissolved into hysterical laughter.

They hugged and laughed and rejoiced until Julia thought she was hugged-out, laughed-out, and rejoiced-out, even though she knew that was impossible with Slavko around.

"I have a surprise, too," Slavko said shyly, his eyes sparkling. "Nothing like commissioning a new Tuba and Violin Concerto, of course. But I hope you'll like it."

"What is it?" Julia said, bouncing up and down in her seat, apparently having caught Slavko's contagious little-kid glee. "Tell me!"

"It isn't as exciting as commissioning a new fiddle-based polka," he said, looking like he was about to burst. "Although I might have to be a copycat and check into that."

"Check into it! Check into it!" Julia said, slipping into the ebullient character of an eight-year-old at Christmas.

"I guess I have to, based on that reaction," Slavko said.

"You have to! You have to!" Julia chanted, giggling.

She waited expectantly.

Slavko just grinned.

"What is it?" Julia said impatiently. "What's your surprise?"

"I guess I can be a tease, too," he said. "I caught that disease from somebody."

Julia swatted his shoulder playfully. "Tell me!"

"I hope you'll like it."

"What is it?"

Slavko reached into his jeans pocket. He dropped to one knee before her and opened a small, square, black felt box. Inside, a gorgeous diamond ring sparkled.

"Julia Chu, will you make me the happiest man alive?" he said. "Will you marry me?"

Julia shrieked for joy. She threw herself into his arms and wrapped herself around him. Six months ago, she never would have said yes to any man. She'd had less than zero interest. It would have taken a gun pointed to her head, and even then, she'd have had to think about it.

But then Slavko came along and everything changed.

She was still *La Petite Rockette*. She still practiced with feverish intensity. Still relentlessly pursued perfection. And still was at the top of the artistic pinnacle.

But with Slavko, she'd found an inner happiness she never thought possible.

She'd found the purest joy and could tell that Slavko had, too.

"Oh my God! Oh my God!" she said over and over, barely choking back the tears, burying her face in his strong shoulder. "I don't believe it!"

She took Slavko's face in her hands, caressed it, and kissed his soft, sweet lips.

"I love you, Slavko!" she said, and then leaned back and shouted to the heavens. "I love Slavko!" And in case the angels and whatever other heavenly beings were up there missed it, she shouted it again and again. "I love Slavko! I love Slavko! I love Slavko!"

Slavko beamed with an even greater happiness than she'd ever seen on his handsome face.

"Is that a yes?" he asked.

The purest joy, profound and true, bubbled up from within Julia's soul and radiated throughout all of her being.

"Commission me that new polka," she said, beaming, "and it's a yes for the rest of our lives!"

About the Author

David H. Hendrickson's first novel, *Cracking the Ice*, was praised by *Booklist* as "a gripping account of a courageous young man rising above evil." He has since published seven additional novels, including *Offside*, which has been adopted for high school student required reading.

His short fiction has appeared in *Best American Mystery Stories 2018*, *Ellery Queen's Mystery Magazine*, *Heart's Kiss*, *Mystery, Crime, and Mayhem*, multiple issues of *Pulphouse*, and numerous anthologies, including over a half dozen issues of *Fiction River*. He is a multi-finalist for the Derringer Award, and his story "Death in the Serengeti" was honored with the 2018 Derringer Award for Best Long Story.

He has published four short story collections: *Shimmers and Laughs: Eight Wildly Hilarious Tales*; *Death in the Serengeti and Other Stories: Ten Tales of Crime*; *The Boy in the Boxers and Other Stories of Sweet Romance*; and *Hell of a Band: Twelve Fantasy Stories*.

Hendrickson has published over fifteen hundred works of nonfiction, most notably his first book for writers, *How to Get Your Book into Schools and Double Your Income with Volume Sales*, and also *Travis Roy: Quadriplegia and a Life of Purpose*. He has been honored with the Joe Concannon Hockey East Media Award and the Murray Kramer Scarlet Quill Award.

Visit him online at www.hendricksonwriter.com.